The Wedding Scratcher

KC McCormick Çiftçi

One

"Remind me never to complain again about traveling out of state for a wedding," Eve grumbled to herself as she tossed clothes into her suitcase. "If I thought driving to Nebraska was a lot of hassle for Clarissa's wedding, it was nothing compared to this. I mean seriously... Istanbul? If I didn't love Celia so much, there is no way I would be flying halfway across the world just to watch her get married."

But it wasn't really the travel that Eve Shields was complaining about. If she was honest with herself, she was excited for the adventure ahead, and she had always wanted to visit Istanbul. She had never been on a trip, for vacation or even traveling to various conferences about software development, that she didn't enjoy.

Her objection was to the idea of traveling for a *wedding*. Because as any of Eve's friends knew, if you wanted to hear one of her signature rants, the best way to ensure it was by bringing up the topic of marriage, and specifically weddings.

"It's not that I'm opposed to marriage," she said to the empty room, as if she were rehearsing for her next happy-hour-soapbox-TED-Talk. "It's about the excess of weddings. All that money spent on one day of your life. One day! Just think of what else you could do with that money. You could make a down payment on a house or take an epic honeymoon for six months." She sighed. "Or, you know, pay off your student loans or donate it all to charity. All better options than spending it on a fancy dress, flowers that will die before you leave for your honeymoon, and an overpriced meal." She threw another black dress into her suitcase, bringing the total number of dresses she had packed so far up to six. While she had enough details from Celia, her oldest friend, to know that some Turkish weddings might last multiple days but that this one would only be one day, that didn't change the fact that she was an indecisive packer and had no way of knowing which particular dress would suit her fancy come the big day.

"The *big day*," she said out loud, following it with a scoff. "How absurd that a phrase like that can only be used to refer to a wedding. Surely we could also use it to refer to, oh, I don't know, the day someone receives their graduate degree or their company goes public or...literally anything else?"

It wouldn't do, having a conversation like this and coming up with such witty one-liners with no one else to hear them. Eve dug around in her pocket and pulled out her phone, dialing the most frequently contacted person in her call history.

"You freaking out about this trip?" was how Simon, her brother, answered his phone. "If it's such a big deal to you, you don't have to go."

"There are so many possible definitions of the phrase 'freaking out,'" she said with a smile, "so let's get specific. I'm not freaking out because I don't know what to pack—"

"Yeah, right," he interrupted. "If you've actually packed a reasonable number of outfits and not packed as if you're planning to do a full costume change every four hours, I owe you a beer."

Eve rolled her eyes, grateful that her little brother couldn't see her. "I'm not even going to address that. As I was saying, though, I'm not 'freaking out' about my wardrobe choices."

"What is it then? The basic concept of committed relationships and matrimony got you down?"

She groaned as she flopped onto her bed, smack in the middle of a pile of discarded clothing that wouldn't be making the journey with her. "Pretty much. Do you realize how much money is spent on the average wedding?"

"I certainly do. If you'll recall, I am, of the two of us, the one who has actually planned a wedding."

"Yeah, but you did it right." Simon had married his high school sweetheart two years before, and their wedding had been the exception to Eve's rules about weddings being a waste of time and money. The celebration had been intimate, just their immediate families and closest friends, and though she hadn't been so bold as to ask just how much money he had spent on the wedding, she was sure it was a fraction of the typical American blowout celebration.

"We did what was right for us," said Simon, "but that doesn't mean it was right for everyone. Lex and I got exactly what we wanted. We wanted to have a small enough number of guests that we would actually be able to spend quality time with everyone and, yeah, we didn't want to spend six months' salary on the whole thing either. But that doesn't mean that everyone else should do it the way we did. If they want to feed the whole community or live out their dreams of dressing up in designer gowns, then who are we to say that they shouldn't? No one is going to be passing any laws about how much money should be spent on a wedding, Eve. Nor should they."

She groaned at that. "I mean, I get that. I'm familiar with the basic concepts of different strokes for different folks and all that."

"Then what, exactly, is the problem?" His tone was indulgent, and Eve was regretting calling him already. She had the sneaking suspicion that he was already considering how he was going to relate this latest misadventure of hers to Lex once the call was over.

"I think I might be having some sort of allergic reaction to the concept of weddings and marriage. Is that a thing?" Simon was a nurse practitioner, after all. He could at least use his medical expertise to help her out.

"It's nothing I've ever heard of before, but you know how science is always evolving and changing our understanding of the human body. I wouldn't rule anything out. What are your symptoms exactly?"

"Well, it's nothing physical, which is why I was confused. It's not the same way I react to pollen or mold, so that's good."

Simon murmured along in agreement, and she exhaled a chuckle. It was fun to joke around with him, almost fun enough to take her mind off the task at hand.

"It's more just...what's the best way to say this?" She paused for just a second for dramatic effect before plowing ahead. "I guess I would sum it up as a strong feeling of aversion. Dread. Annoyance. The temptation to lie down on the floor and bang my fists and kick my heels and throw a proper tantrum, two-year-old style."

"Well, that does sound serious."

She nodded. "It does. So, you see, I really don't think I should be getting on a plane any time soon. My body is literally rejecting even the idea of going to this wedding, and what kind of hypocrite would I be if I—"

"Eve, no." Simon's tone had some impact behind it as he interrupted her. "You're being ridiculous. First of all, this is Celia. You love Celia. We all love Celia. And if you don't go and support her—and represent the entire Shields family, might I add—then you will regret it. Not just because you will naturally feel bad about standing up your oldest friend, but because I will make *sure* you feel bad about it every chance I get."

"What else?" she asked through gritted teeth. "You said 'first of all,' so..."

"Right." Simon was plowing ahead, and she could almost picture him pacing through his kitchen as he spoke. "Second of all, it's Istanbul. Do you know how cool it's going to be to explore Istanbul? If we looked alike, I'd steal your passport and go in your place."

"Ah, but alas," said Eve with a genuine smile. "Curse these darn genes of ours that would never let us pull that off. It would never work."

"Not even if I shaved?" Simon was sporting a full ginger beard these days, but even with a shave and a brown wig, it was clear that he took after their mother while Eve was more like a mini female version of their father.

"Trust me, I wish we could do that even more than you do." She sighed. "But just...well, hypothetically, why don't you tell me what you'd be so excited to see and do in Istanbul just in case, you know...it isn't already on my list." Eve knew enough about Istanbul to know that it had its fair share of history and culture, but when it came to specifics, the list of sights to see was surprisingly short, and the last thing she wanted to do was clue her brother in to that fact. Sure, it was on her to-do list—once she actually resigned herself to the fact that this trip was happening—to pull together some sort of itinerary, but she hadn't exactly gotten around to it yet.

"Seriously, Eve?" Her brother sighed into the phone. "I mean, where do I even begin? There's the fact that the city has an Asian side and a European side, which is, like, way cooler than going to the Four Corners on a family road trip and having one of your family members stand in each state and carrying on about it like it's the coolest thing ever—"

"Hey!" Eve cut in. "That *was* cool, and I was also eight years old. It's not like we took that trip last year."

Simon laughed. "No, we certainly didn't. Though it would be a little harder to get Mom and Dad to take a road trip with us these days."

Eve winced. Their parents had separated in the past year, after thirty years of marriage, and the thought of it still brought a pang to her chest, even after countless hours dissecting it with her therapist. It wasn't as if Elaine and George Shields had been living the picture of American sitcom domestic bliss, but they had seemed happy. Of course, as Eve looked back at the last few years now, there was a marked shift in the tone of their family gatherings. While in the past they had been more inclined to laugh together about the stupid thing the dog was doing, in more recent years, it seemed like her parents had been doing more laughing *at* each other than *with* each other.

There was also the fact that both of her parents had separately confided in Eve since the separation began a version of the same thing. *He thinks I'm a fool*, her mom had said, *and I'm sick of it*. Her dad, on the other hand, had shaken his head sadly. *She just doesn't respect me any more, and I'm tired of being the punchline of every joke.*

On second thought, maybe they were *more like the typical sitcom family than she had originally thought*, thought Eve, as images from her childhood television viewing flashed through her mind. The "I hate my wife" and "My husband is the worst" jokes had been a nearly ubiquitous part of her experience of growing up.

"You still there?" Simon's voice broke through her reverie. "Sorry for bordering on the edge of The Subject Which Shall Not Be Named. It just slipped out."

"No, it's okay," said Eve, letting her guard slip for just a second. "It might actually be good for the two of us to try talking about it again. I think-slash-hope that I've done enough processing by now to not run out of the room like a dramatic, emotional teenager." She let out a humorless laugh. "No promises though."

"And I promise not to try to Parent Trap Mom and Dad. Or, actually, not even to suggest it. They're going to do whatever makes sense for them, and I promise to do my best to accept it."

Eve narrowed her eyes as she surveyed her open suitcase. "Are you holding your fingers up in that scout's honor gesture?"

"It's better than crossing them behind my back," said Simon, "but yes. Yes, I am. I am solemnly vowing to let my parents be humans and not insist they only be parents who do what they think is right for the children."

"Yeah, I mean..." Eve blew out a breath, her lips fluttering as she did so. "It's a bad enough idea to stay together for the kids when the kids are...you know, *actual* kids. But when the kids are old enough to start thinking about saving for retirement, it really doesn't make sense."

"Hey now." Simon sounded put out, and that made Eve smile. "Just because some of us are being responsible and thinking about the future, that doesn't mean we aren't still young and cool and fun and all of those things."

"Hmm." She paused in thought. "I feel a bit ancient at the moment. Like ten years ago, I would have been throwing my best party dresses in a bag and hitchhiking to the airport, and now—"

"Hold up," Simon interrupted. "Mom would never have let you do that ten years ago. You would have been 17, Eve. I think you meant something more like two years ago, and that definitely does weaken your point. Also, there is no chance any of your friends were getting married ten years ago, thank God. Very grateful we all managed to get to the other side of our adolescence without anyone needing to get a note from their parents granting them permission to get married before they were 18."

"All perfectly valid points," Eve admitted, an uncomfortable feeling forming in the pit of her stomach. "Are you suggesting, perhaps, that I might have been more excited about a wedding two years ago than I am now because...oh, I don't know...two years ago I still thought our parents were happily married?"

She could practically hear him shrug into the phone. "I don't know, Eve. I'm not that kind of doctor."

"You're not a doctor at all, dumbass," she scoffed.

"Right, but I'm definitely not *that* kind of doctor, in addition to already not being a doctor. You know what I mean?"

"You're ridiculous. Are you telling me that if you were on this flight with me and someone started having a medical emergency and they asked if there was a doctor on board, you would raise your hand and give an impromptu speech about the difference between MDs and nurse practitioners before finding out if there was actually anything helpful you could do?"

"I don't know, sis," said Simon, and she felt a twinge of nervous anticipation. He only called her "sis" when he was about to drop a bomb.

"What?" she asked, waiting with bated breath for him to continue.

"Oh, nothing. Just sounds to me like you're already committed to getting on that flight of yours. You didn't say *if* I go or anything like that. You said if I came with you. I kind of stopped listening after that, so whatever sick burn you attempted to deliver, it didn't reach me. Wrong address, I guess."

She groaned in exasperation. "Of course I'm going, Simon. I was never *not* going, no matter how much I may not want to."

"Yeah?" He sounded genuinely shocked. "What was the point of this whole call, then?"

"Apparently, it wasn't to talk me into anything," she said through gritted teeth. "Apparently, it was for me to talk through my feelings and feel held and supported so that I could arrive on the other side with a packed suitcase and just the tiniest bit of excitement about my upcoming adventure."

"Ah. So I failed fairly epically at that, huh? I'm guessing you weren't looking to be reminded of our parents' impending divorce or—"

"You don't know that they're getting divorced, so don't say it like it's a foregone conclusion."

"Right. Still, though, you probably didn't want your little rant about weddings being a waste of money to turn into questioning the viability of a long-term relationship in any capacity." He let out one single laugh then. "Who would have known that the lessons of couples therapy would apply to your relationship with your sister, too?"

Eve felt the blood drain from her face as if in slow motion. "Couples therapy?" She gritted her teeth. "What's wrong? What's going on? What can I do to help? What did you do wrong?"

"Chill, Eve, it's okay."

"It is not okay, not if you and Lex are in counseling." She stopped herself from saying out loud that she could not handle another close relationship in her inner circle falling apart, remembering just as the words were about to escape unheeded that this was likely much more traumatic for her brother than it could possibly be for her.

"Believe it or not," he began, "but we aren't actually in therapy to address a problem. And I know that celebrities say that all the time and no one ever believes them, but it's actually true." He paused then as he took a deep breath. "It's just that when Mom and Dad announced the separation, it really shocked me. Just like it shocked you. And Lex and I, we wanted to make sure we were on the right track. That we were already doing the right things to ensure the firmest foundation for our marriage. I intend to love that woman for the rest of my life, so I'm not taking any chances where it comes to her."

"Simon, that..." Eve glanced down to see that she had placed her hand on her heart, touched by her brother's words and his dedication to his wife. "That's really sweet," she said. "And I hope you said exactly that to her."

"Oh, I did. I do, actually. I say something to that effect at least once a day. I just, apparently, missed the part where what works in one relationship could be helpful in another one."

"Oh, right," said Eve, remembering how the topic had come up. "What did you mean? I could use all the relationship tips I can get."

"Says the most single person I know," said Simon, stifling his words with a badly timed cough. "But the point is about clarifying what someone wants rather than delivering what you think they need."

Before she could ask him to clarify what he meant, he plowed on.

"I mean, when Lex comes to me with a frustration from her day, I know now to ask if she is looking for solutions or just wants to be heard. But with you, I could have done the same sort of thing. Asked if you were looking to be talked into a trip you didn't actually want to take, or if you just wanted to vent some frustration. I'll try to remember that for next time."

"Right." Eve paused then, shocked into silence. "So when exactly did you get replaced with such a convincing clone of yourself?"

"Sorry, sis." She could hear the smile in his voice. "If it's not too late to ask, what did you actually need from me on this fine evening? Could I interest you in a listening ear? A nonjudgmental observer? Or would you prefer the two of us rant about our distaste for weddings together?"

She laughed at that. "I think I already got what I needed, Simon. Thanks for renewing my faith in the male species ever so slightly, and for giving me a little bit of perspective about this impending trip of mine."

"So you're definitely going then? And maybe even feeling a tiny bit of excitement about it?"

Eve nodded. "I was always going, but yeah. Now I'm at least aware that a chance to explore Istanbul is better than staying put at home and playing therapist to my parents as their marriage falls apart."

Simon snorted. "The fact that you were able to lose sight of that particular truth for even a moment is truly astounding. But yeah, you definitely are getting the better end of that particular deal." He let out a shuddering breath. "I can only hope they don't increase their frequency of calls to me in your absence."

"You could always come with me, you know..."

He sighed. "I would if I could. At least one of the Shields siblings isn't allergic to fun."

Two

"I can't believe you're actually coming!" Celia's face filled the screen of Eve's phone, her excitement spilling through the phone and across the miles. Eve tossed up a quick murmur of gratitude to some wiser version of herself that had reminded her to put on her headphones before making the call, aware that airports may not have the same expectations of calm and quiet as, say, a library, but that certain levels of exuberance were appropriate only in the privacy of one's own home.

"Of course I'm coming," said Eve, keeping her voice at an appropriate volume so as not to disturb her fellow travelers. "When did I ever give you even the slightest indication that I wasn't coming? Do you really think I would miss your wedding?"

Celia waved a dismissive hand at the screen. "I don't mean it like that. I always knew you were coming, even if we both know you're a bit of a curmudgeon at heart when it comes to weddings. But no, I mean...like...well, you're *coming*! Today! The day is finally here that my oldest friend is traveling across the world to come help me get ready for my wedding!" She shook her head in disbelief. "And the wedding itself is going to be here before we even know it!"

"Yeah." Eve spoke through gritted teeth. After some cajoling on Celia's part and some behind-the-scenes guilt tripping from Simon, Eve had agreed to arrive in Istanbul two weeks early to help Celia get ready for the big day. Her software development job was flexible enough that it didn't much matter where her tasks were completed but only that they were, in fact, completed, and so her boss hadn't batted an eye or even required her to use any of her paid time off for the trip.

It was a sweet deal, and Eve knew it, but that wasn't enough to overcome the grumpiness that always accompanied a long day of travel. "Remind me again of how I'm supposed to be helpful to you," she grumbled. "It's not like I have any wedding-related contacts in Turkey." She held up a finger and then added another one to it. "And it's also not as if I can understand a single word of Turkish. I really hope you're calling me in for support more in the emotional or metaphorical sense and not in the sense where you actually expect me to be any help at all."

Celia chuckled at that, losing herself for a moment in the mirth. When she was finished laughing, she shook her head as she wiped her eyes. "As it turns out," she began, "I am not calling in my oldest and dearest friend in the hopes that she knows the best cake maker and wedding boutique in Istanbul two weeks before my wedding." She shook her head again. "If you can believe it, most of the details for the big day are already sorted out, actually. I mean, I'm going to need your help figuring out one thing with the photographer, but that's it. I swear." She held up a hand as if in protection from whatever Eve was about to fling in her direction. "Apart from that, it's just, well...you know. It's nice to have someone from my side here, too. I know a lot of them will be here for the actual wedding, but I can't wait that long to have a little representation from the American contingent."

"Well, I'm honored that you asked me, and I'm glad I can be there for you." Eve smiled then, and she felt her heart lift at the happiness so evident on her friend's face. There was no way she could have missed this, no part of her that would have been comfortable sitting out an event that was creating so much joy in her friend's life. "I wouldn't miss it," she said.

"Oh, you're absolutely right about that," said Celia with a resolute nod. "I would have flown over there and dragged you back here by the scruff of your neck like a...well, like a naughty kitten, I guess."

Eve raised an eyebrow. "Is that...a common comparison? Can't say I've ever heard it before."

Celia shrugged. "Who even knows anymore? You have to remember that I live with a vet and my life revolves around cats now." She held up a brown tabby that must have been sitting on her lap just out of view of the camera. She kissed the animal repeatedly on the top of its head before seemingly becoming aware of Eve's silent presence on the other end of the phone line.

"I...uh, are you a cat person?" The cat disappeared from view with a small sound of protest, and Celia's face grew in size as she leaned closer to the camera. "I don't know why I don't know that about you. Badem naps in the guest room sometimes, but I'm going to change all the linens before you come and keep the door closed."

"No, it's okay." Eve forced a smile as the image of a black and white kitten flashed through her mind unbidden. "I like cats, and I'm sure Badem and I will get along like old friends."

"Good." Celia's relief was evident. "With some people, like my uncle who's allergic to cats, it's the perfect excuse not to have him come stay for a visit. But I would hate it if that were the case for you. I could have her go stay with the neighbors, but even if I hired, like, the fixers who remove all the evidence from crime scenes, there would still be cat hair around here."

"No, no. Seriously." Now it was Eve making a placating gesture. "I doubt my little cat niece would ever forgive me if I kicked her out of her own house, and I would have a hard time living with myself, too. If anything, the two of us will probably end up having a girls' night and stay up late painting our nails and eating cat treats."

"You sure do know how to party," said Celia with a nod. "If I'm invited, I'll join you for part of that, but I think I would prefer popcorn to cat treats. Could that be arranged?"

"We'll see. I'll have to talk it over with Badem, of course." Eve chuckled then. "I really am excited to see you. To meet Enes and Badem. And to have you show me around your new city, too, of course."

"You're going to love it," said Celia, and she said it so confidently that Eve couldn't help but believe her.

Three

T he first views of Istanbul snuck up on Eve. She had lost herself in the world of '90s rom-coms, thrilled to discover that the airline offered a vast selection of new and old movies to pass the time. While her curmudgeonly ways did sometimes extend to referring to new music as "noise" and new movies as lacking the depth and humor of the old standbys from her youth, she was nothing if not a diehard fan of every movie Sandra Bullock had ever made. And the entertainment system on the back of the seat in front of her had five movies that fit that particular description, and so she committed herself to working her way through all of them.

There was a part of her that wondered what would be left for her to enjoy on her flight back to St. Louis in a few weeks. But that was what Meg Ryan was for, and she wouldn't say no to another movie marathon when the opportunity presented.

And so, she was just getting to the major reveal in *Miss Congeniality* when the pilot announced they would be beginning their descent into Istanbul and that it was time to open all the window shades and return their seats to their full, upright position. She opened her window, put up her tray, adjusted her seat...and kept watching her movie. It was only a few moments later, when they had broken through the clouds, that she glanced to her side and gasped audibly.

"Holy—!"

The woman sitting next to her jerked her head in her direction. "What? Is there a problem? Is it the wing?"

"No!" Eve was pointing out the window now. "It's Istanbul! Look at it, it's amazing!"

The woman sitting next to her shook her head and turned away, muttering something under her breath about, "Of course it's Istanbul. Where did she think she was going, Toronto?"

But it was easy for Eve to ignore her seat partner. Minarets dotted the horizon throughout the city, a view unlike anything she'd ever seen on approach before. It was incredible, immediately forcing her to recalibrate her expectations for just how epic this trip of hers was going to be. Wedding or not, the fact was that she was about to be exiting the airport into one of the more intriguing cities she had ever learned about.

She had spent the days since her pep talk with Simon reading up on Turkey in general and Istanbul in particular, and she had found herself surprised time and time again by all the natural beauty the country had to offer. If she had more time—if there weren't an entire wedding to prepare for—she might have enjoyed the opportunity to explore more of the country. Whether that was wandering through the misty highlands of the Black Sea region that were so reminiscent of Scotland or parking herself on a beach lounger on the Mediterranean or Aegean coasts, she was surprised to admit that she would have said yes to it all.

Maybe there are more trips to Turkey in my future, she wondered as she stared out the window at the approaching airport. She felt the strangest sort of premonition, as if this were only the first of many times she would be arriving in the city like this, already knowing that her current level of excitement would be the norm.

"Well, that was weird," she mumbled to herself, shaking off the feeling. As a rule, Eve wasn't a particularly suspicious person, and she didn't put much stock in any way of "knowing" something that didn't center entirely around her head. Whatever she was feeling about Turkey at the moment wasn't a premonition. It was wishful thinking, plain and simple. She was excited to be exploring a new city, and that meant she already wanted to prolong that excitement—and what better way to do that than to extend its borders from Istanbul to the entire country?

By the time the plane had landed and Eve had made her way to the other side of passport control and customs, baggage in hand, her excitement had dissipated slightly, replaced by hunger, exhaustion, and the desperate wish for a shower. As thrilling as a new adventure might be, it didn't supplant the needs of the body or Eve's lifelong distaste for standing in lines.

As she made her final exit from the airport, her eyes landed on a familiar face and she felt her muscles relax at the sight of it. If her shoulders had worked their way up around her ears as she had tried to make her way smoothly through the airport and choose the quickest line every time, the mere presence of Celia Long was enough to make them drop in relief.

"Celia!" she cried as she jogged the last few steps into her friend's outstretched arms. "Oh my gosh, it's so good to see you!" She pulled back and shook her head as she gestured around them. "I can't believe I'm really here!"

"I can't believe it either!" Celia pulled her back in for another hug, which turned into a bouncing one this time as the smaller woman began to jump, propelling Eve to do the same. "I've missed you so much and I'm so happy that you're here that I could just..." She trailed off for a moment before speaking again. "Well honestly, I could just take a nap snuggled up next to you on the couch with the air conditioner blasting." She released her friend and stepped back. "I'm honestly just so tired of all this wedding stuff and having you here feels like I can let go of all of that and just...*blah*." She slumped her shoulders and jutted out her chin in a way that seemed like she was melting on her feet, and Eve had to laugh.

"If I didn't know you so well and know that was probably the highest compliment you could give, I'd be offended." She slung one arm across Celia's shoulders. "But the fact that your nervous system relaxes in my presence is not an honor I take lightly. And of course, the feeling is mutual, except—" She pulled her arm away from her friend, lifting it to take a slight sniff before replacing it at her side. "Well, I definitely need to take a shower. Wash the travel off of me."

Celia was nodding. "And we need to get some food in you too, of course. Are you hungry?" She reached for Eve's suitcase and nodded towards the lines of cars. "Let's go load up the car."

"Is your man here?" Eve asked, wrinkling her nose as she tried to peer into the dark windows of the cars they passed. "He didn't want to come meet me fresh off the plane?"

Celia shook her head. "He didn't want to make the initial reunion about him, actually. He thought there might be...well, I don't know. Maybe tears? Maybe we would have just sobbed in joy at the sight of each other and that would have been embarrassing for you in front of someone you hadn't even met yet?" She shrugged. "I told him it was totally unnecessary, but at least this way we get some nice curbside service."

She nodded towards a car that was pulling to a stop in front of them now, a smile spreading across her face as a handsome, dark-haired man with a broad smile slid out of his seatbelt and jumped out of the driver's seat so quickly that Eve worried for a second that he hadn't even put the car in park.

"You must be Eve!" he cried as he came around to greet them, holding out his arms.

Eve stepped into the circle of his arms, fully prepared to give the most cursory of hugs and then pleasantly surprised at the warmth and sincerity conveyed by his quick but snug embrace. "Guilty as charged," she said as she pulled back. "And you must be Enes."

He smiled and nodded. "I certainly am. But it would have been a good joke if I had said I wasn't, wouldn't it?" He looked at Celia, nodding with a hopeful expression in his eyes. "I could have pretended to be someone else. Like a really friendly taxi driver or..."

As he trailed off in thought, Celia stepped towards him and put an arm around his waist, the smile she gave him telling Eve everything she needed to know about just how smitten her friend was. "It all would have been hilarious, love," Celia was telling Enes, "but I'm guessing Eve will be a little more receptive to your jokes when she's a little less jet lagged and a little more..." She glanced at her friend, raising an eyebrow. "Fed, watered, and has slept for ten hours?"

Eve nodded. "And don't forget about the shower. That's important, too."

"Of course." Enes was making quick work of placing her bags in the trunk of the car, nodding all the while. "We will make a few stops then, on the way back to the apartment." He looked at both women in turn for confirmation. "I'm guessing now is not the time for any exploring or sight seeing. We will stop for some sustenance and take it back home? We can take Eve out somewhere nice later if she feels up for it or just wait until tomorrow?"

Celia was looking at her friend with raised eyebrows, and Eve nodded. "That sounds great. As much as I wish I could be the kind of person to hop off a plane and go straight into the heart of the city, soaking it all up..."

"Say no more," said Celia, with a hand raised. She gestured towards herself and Enes. "If anyone understands the importance of getting comfy and cozy, it's us. It's really good that you're here not only because I adore you, but also because it will force us to get out of the house a little more these days."

Eve chuckled as she shook her head at Celia's offer of the passenger seat, opting to slide into the backseat. She was enjoying observing the dynamic between Celia and Enes too much not to give herself a front-row seat, and sitting in the front but turning around to talk to her friend was nothing but a great way to tweak her neck or activate her motion sickness. "So you two aren't party animals?" she asked the couple in mock disbelief. "You aren't going to show me the best nightclubs Istanbul has to offer?"

"If that is what you want, we will take you there," said Enes, the picture of sincerity. "It's not generally how we spend our evenings, but we want you to have a great time." He leaned forward slightly in his seat to make eye contact with her in the rearview mirror. "I'm probably not supposed to tell you this, but we're hoping you'll have such a good time in Istanbul that you'll want to come back." He darted a glance in Celia's direction. "I suspect my beautiful bride's secret wish is that you'll be in town quite often. Or that maybe you'd even move here."

Celia shook her head at him, chuckling softly. "Great work, love. Way to plant the seeds."

Enes shrugged. "What can I say? If I know there's something you want, I'm going to try my best to get it for you. What, was I supposed to leave subliminal messages around for Eve to try to convince her? I don't even know how that works. I'm a vet, not a professional best friend manipulator."

"Don't tell him I said this," Celia stage whispered over her shoulder to Eve, "but I'm not even sure 'best friend manipulator' is a real job." She gave her friend a gasp of mock horror before turning back to the front, reaching a reassuring hand across to pat Enes on the knee. "You did great, love. And hey, if it works, then who am I to question your tactics?"

Enes was looking at Eve again in the mirror. "So?" he asked. "Did it work? Are you thinking of moving to Istanbul or at least taking a vacation here a couple of times a year?" He gestured briefly to the road they were traveling on, buildings whizzing by on both sides. "What do you think so far?"

She laughed at that. "I think it's too soon to tell, but I will definitely take it into consideration." She bit her tongue to keep from telling them about the feeling she had had as the plane landed, her premonition of sorts. If she didn't even believe in it, then it wouldn't be fair to tell Celia and get her hopes up.

Four

They made a couple of stops on the way back to Enes and Celia's apartment, but the two women stayed in the car, chatting and catching up while Enes ran their errands.

"I insist," he had said at the final stop. "This is no way for Eve to get her first impression of Istanbul."

"Technically," she called from the back seat, "I already got my first impression of Istanbul. From the air, I mean." She smiled at Celia. "I thought it was really pretty."

"Yes, but there is a difference between looking at the city from higher than a bird's-eye view and actually walking on its streets," said Enes. "Though if you would like to walk around on these streets, you are certainly welcome to. Don't let me stop you. I only thought you would prefer to eat and nap and shower…" He looked at Celia for confirmation, and she nodded. "Right," he replied. "I will do my part to make that happen, then. Food it is!"

As he slammed the door behind him, Celia turned to her friend with a look of expectation and a raised eyebrow. "So," she said, "what do you think?"

"Of Istanbul?" asked Eve, playing dumb. "I think I already told you it's too soon—"

"You know I'm not talking about Istanbul," Celia interrupted. "Enes! This is your first time meeting him..."

"Right," said Eve with a slow nod, "and yet it doesn't feel like that at all. Don't forget, I've been hearing you talk about him for over a year now, and I've met him on video calls at least, like, ten times."

"Ah, yeah." Celia exhaled something like a laugh through her nose. "That's true. So I guess you like him, then?"

Eve laughed at that. "No, not at all," she deadpanned. "I flew thousands of miles because I don't like your husband-to-be." She leaned forward and placed a hand on Celia's shoulder. "But really, though, I have never seen you this happy. It's like...well, it's like I'm meeting a new version of you that I never knew. But I really like her. She seems...peaceful, I guess? There's something very comfortable about the two of you, and I mean that in the best possible way."

Celia narrowed her eyes at her friend. "You don't mean that we just got old and boring in our settled ways, do you? We sort of both did turn into cat ladies, after all."

Eve snorted. "Yeah, and you were such a party animal before. No, I'm really concerned about you, babe. I'm just so worried that you aren't going to want to do shots with me and dance to bad club remixes while a bunch of sweaty people gyrate around us."

"Right." Celia nodded. "So it isn't just me who is uninterested in night life."

"Some things never change, babe. Staying in on a Friday night as a college student to drink tea and watch the BBC miniseries of *Pride and Prejudice* in its entirety should have clued both of us in to some key facts about our personalities."

Celia smiled warmly. "I have so much affection for that version of myself. She really didn't give a damn what anyone else thought about her." She shook her head. "Of course, that didn't stop me from going through a phase or two where I tried to be who I thought I was supposed to be..." She sniffed. "Still, I'm glad I found my way back to her."

"Me, too," said Eve. "For both of us, I mean. And yet, as much as I wish I could time travel and tell my younger self not to care so much about what other people think..."

"...you know she would never have listened to you?" asked Celia, with a twinkle in her eyes.

"Not even a little bit," said Eve with a nod. "And I'm sure there are things I'm doing and believing now that some future version of me will find fault with." She shrugged. "That's the nature of existence, I guess. You live your life thinking you have it all figured out, only to find out in the very near future that everything about you is cringeworthy."

Celia shook her head. "Best to keep moving forward then, huh? If you cringe too much, your face might freeze that way."

Enes returned then with a bulging bag, the smell of which instantly made Eve's mouth water. "Let's get home!" he exclaimed, throwing the car into gear as soon as his seatbelt was secured and—from Eve's vantage point in the backseat, at least—narrowly stopping himself from peeling out as he drove away.

Celia and Enes's neighborhood was cute, full of tall, old buildings in a variety of colors and a smattering of trees. A few cats milled around, and Eve smiled to herself as she pictured Celia's life here.

As they unloaded Eve's things from the car, Enes grabbed one suitcase and Celia held onto the other bag with a death grip, insisting that Eve didn't need to lift a finger.

"I can carry my own bags, you know," she said, crossing her arms over her chest. "I managed to get this far without having the two of you there to do all the heavy lifting."

"Exactly," said Enes with a nod that conveyed a sense of finality. "You've carried them long enough, and now it's time for you to share that pleasure with us."

"Plus," added Celia, "there's no elevator in the building and we're on the fourth floor."

Eve held up her hands. "Okay, then. No more argument from me."

As they began to walk towards the building, Celia nodded towards a tree. "That's where I first met Badem." Then she tilted her head towards the door of the building. "And that's where I met Enes."

"Oh wow, so this is going to be like a guided tour of your first days in Istanbul?" Eve stopped in her tracks, trying to take it all in before shaking her head. "I'm trying to picture it, but I just can't. Let me guess." She lifted a hand to stroke her chin. "You chased the cat up the tree and then Enes came out and scolded you?"

Celia chuckled at that, but it was Enes who spoke up. "You got it almost right, in that you got everything exactly wrong." His smile was broad, his eyes creasing at the corners as the memory took hold of him. "Badem was up in the tree trying to trick Celia into thinking she was stuck there, and I approached after that whole fiasco was over, when the two of them were falling in love. I believe Celia was feeding Badem at the time, and Badem, in return, was plotting how she would dart inside the building and then inside Celia's apartment and that she would never sleep outside again."

Celia had been watching him as he spoke, her smile mirroring his. "And that was the beginning of a series of awkward encounters with Enes, where he would either catch me talking to cats—"

"She didn't know yet that I also talk to cats. I mean, it's practically my job," he interjected.

"Or he would find me stalking around the building in my pajamas looking for Badem," Celia continued. "I'm fairly convinced now that our entire relationship was part of her master plan. Badem, apparently, wanted to have two cat parents."

They had opened the front door of the building, and Eve slipped in behind Celia as Enes held the door. "Sounds like you have your own little matchmaker," said Eve, glancing at Celia and Enes in turn. "Is she going to have some kind of special role at the wedding? Maybe make a speech, or at least be the ring bearer?"

"Badem is very attached to Celia," said Enes as they began to climb the stairs. "But she is also a cat, which means she follows directions on her own terms. If we put the ring on a collar around her neck, she might follow Celia right down the aisle to deliver it, or she might demonstrate her tree climbing abilities again."

"She'll be at home for the wedding," said Celia. "Or maybe over at Jasmine's apartment, having the cat version of a play date with Cheddar. That's where they eat and nap together."

"That sounds shockingly similar to my idea of a good time," said Eve, and she heard Enes chuckle behind her.

Celia pointed towards a door they were passing. "This is my old apartment, where I lived when I first moved her. Meredith is there now, and you'll meet her soon. Jasmine, too." She smiled over her shoulder at Eve. "We've got a great little community in this building."

"Celia, my dear." Enes's voice sounded from over Eve's shoulder, a playful tint of warning in it. "Remember that you aren't supposed to try to convince Eve to move here yet." He dropped his voice to a stage whisper. "So definitely don't tell her anything about the empty apartment across from Meredith's, okay?"

Eve shook her head as she chuckled softly. "Don't you two know it's a bad idea to make decisions when you're sleep deprived?" She darted a glance between them. "Or is that exactly what you're trying to do since my guard is down and I'm more likely to be impulsive? I'm telling you right now, I won't sign a lease today. Probably not even tomorrow, either. Let's not forget that I have a return ticket back to St. Louis, as well as a job waiting for me there."

They had arrived in front of a door, where Celia was turning a key in the lock. She stopped mid turn and looked at her friend over her shoulder, leveling the kind of glare that conveyed the full extent of how much she saw through all of Eve's words.

"You're a software developer, Eve. You can work from anywhere. You're working remotely for two weeks when you're here, and you go into the office only when you feel like it. That job is the last thing calling you back to Missouri. I'm not saying I won't accept *any* objection to your moving to Istanbul, just that I won't accept that particular one."

"Good to know," said Eve, but she was smiling. "I have to say, you move fast, Celia. Twenty minutes ago we were talking about the possibility of me visiting Istanbul more and now we're already shooting down reasons why I can't move here."

"You don't know the half of it," said Enes. "She and Badem moved in together the first day they met."

As if summoned by the sound of her name, the door slipped open and a brown tabby materialized in the opening, stepping into the hallway where she was immediately scooped up into Celia's arms.

"And who could blame me for that?" asked Celia, kissing the cat's head as loud purring began to sound. "It was love at first sight, and there wasn't anything I could do about it." She turned to face Eve, who held out her hand for Badem to sniff.

"This is, obviously, Badem," said Celia, hugging the cat a little closer. "And Badem, this is my friend, Eve. I think you two are going to get along famously."

Eve reached forward and lightly clasped the paw dangling closest to her. "A pleasure to meet you, Badem."

Badem gave her a small chirping sound in response, and then the four of them made their way into the apartment.

Five

Celia showed Eve to her bedroom before getting her set up with a towel and toiletries to freshen up. "You can shower now, or we can eat first. It's up to you, to whatever is the more pressing concern."

"A shower then," said Eve before grimacing. "That won't be a problem for the food, will it? I don't want everything to get cold because of me."

"Not a problem at all." Celia shook her head. "Enes will probably have already put it all in the oven to keep it warm. He's good like that."

Eve smiled at her friend. "It's really nice to see you like this," she said, the words slipping out unguarded. "I mean, just...well, the idea that you have someone else who picks up the slack. Someone who's on your team and he's taking care of the food while you're showing me around. You don't have to do it all yourself."

"Of course," said Celia, a funny expression crossing her face. "That's how a relationship is supposed to work, isn't it?"

"Well, it's the first I'm hearing of the concept," said Eve with a shrug. "I mean, that isn't fair to Simon and Lex. I'm sure they have a great relationship. But it's not like I stay at their house that often, seeing as we live so close to each other."

Celia nodded with understanding. "Your parents?"

"Bingo," said Eve. "That was a constant refrain growing up, about how she felt like everything was her responsibility and he never helped her." She tilted her head to the side. "Of course, my dad complained about all the financial pressure he was under. I think they both felt like they were the one shouldering all the burden and no one realized just how much the other person was actually doing." She gave a sad smile. "They could have been great teammates, and life could have been a lot easier if they had only realized they were fighting to accomplish the same goal."

Celia was quiet, looking contemplative as she nodded slowly. "You're quite profound when you're jet lagged. Did you know that?"

Eve smiled. "What do you think? Should I call my parents right now, get them on a video call and give them a little counseling session?" She held up her towel. "Or should I keep my great ideas to myself and see what else I can come up with during a little shower brainstorming session?"

Celia pointed to the towel. "I'm choosing that one."

"I'm barely stopping myself from doing a sniff test to find out why you chose that particular option," said Eve, "but I do appreciate the honesty." She lifted her towel and marched in the direction of the bathroom. "Off to perform imaginary therapy on my parents in the shower!"

She stopped and turned to face Celia. "Can we just pretend I never said that?" She shivered as she slunk off to the bathroom.

Six

By the time Eve had showered and eaten, she felt like a new woman. She leaned back against the couch, smiling as her eyebrows climbed her forehead in surprise as Badem jumped up onto her lap.

"Oh my gosh, is this really happening? Already?" She looked to Celia, who was smiling back at her.

"It looks like it," said Celia, "but you know how cats are. Don't count your chickens until they're hatched or... well, don't say there's a cat on your lap until she's actually there."

And then, as if Celia's words had spoken it into existence, Badem accepted one last pat on the head from Eve and then stepped off her lap, walking the few feet that separated her from Celia before curling up easily on her lap, her eyes closing as soon as her chin hit her paw.

"I see how it is," said Eve, "but I swear I'm not mad. I'll win her over before my time here is up. Just you wait and see."

"I don't doubt that you will," said Celia, serenely stroking the cat's head. "So," she began, looking up at her friend. "How are you feeling now? Do you want to lie low today, or would it feel good to get out and walk a bit?"

Eve was already nodding. "I would love to stretch my legs, and I'm sure I'll sleep better tonight if I do. Why? Do you have something in mind, or should we just wander around and see what happens?"

Celia pulled a face. "Well, first of all, please know that you aren't obligated to come along for this just because you said you were free. It isn't like someone asking what you're doing this weekend and then saying, 'Great, you can help me move!' and you don't have any way to get out of it."

"Right." Eve shook her head. "The great thing about jet lag is that it will be my go-to 'get out of anything I don't want to do' card for the next two weeks. Even when it no longer makes sense for me to have jet lag, even when I have slept for a full thirteen hours and am well adjusted to Turkey Time...even then I reserve the right to play the jet lag card when I don't want to do something."

"That's good to know," said Celia, rolling her eyes. "So now every time you tell me you're tired, I will just assume that you actually don't want to do whatever I asked you."

"Shit." Eve shook her head. "I did kind of shoot myself in the foot with that one, didn't I?" She sighed. "Anyway, what was it that you were going to ask me to do that I may or may not be too tired to do?"

Celia smiled. "I'm just teasing you, by the way. There isn't actually anything wrong with saying no just because you don't feel like doing something. Even to me."

"Even to you?" Eve shook her head. "No, it's one thing to say no to a dumb idea from my brother or even a project from my boss that doesn't make sense. To my best friend, well, that's a whole different ball game."

Celia raised an eyebrow. "That makes it all the more important. It isn't particularly impressive if you're only good at saying no to people when it's an established dynamic in your relationship, like with your brother. But if you hesitate to say no to me, then maybe that means you aren't sure we'll be cool if you do something I don't like." She reached an arm over, dropping her hand on Eve's knee. "So, at least by the end of your visit here, I hope you'll be confident enough in our friendship that you'll be able to say no without worrying that you've fundamentally changed things between us."

"Is that your whole goal for this visit? I mean, apart from getting married, obviously."

"Something like that," said Celia, but her grin was broad. At the mention of her upcoming wedding to Enes, her eyes wandered to him, where he was washing the last few dishes in the kitchen.

Eve cleared her throat to call her friend back to the moment, a rush of discomfort at the unguarded moment, at the intimacy that felt as foreign to her as the city outside the apartment walls. "So what was it you wanted to do?"

"Right!" Celia clapped her hands, which earned her a reproachful look from Badem, who was jostled awake at the sound. "I need to go to the venue where the wedding is going to be. I've been there a few times already, but we're trying to figure out the dessert tables." She pulled a face again. "If you don't want to come, I swear you don't have to. It'll probably be boring, but if all you want is to get a few steps in, then it should do the trick."

Eve turned in her seat to face her friend. "Need I remind you that I came here to help with your wedding? Doesn't this sound like exactly the sort of task that would fall under that general umbrella?"

"Oh, it definitely does." Celia nodded. "The problem is that there is another umbrella for all the 'tasks that remind Eve of what a hassle and scam weddings are.'" She raised her hands to make quotation marks around the phrase. "And those two umbrellas don't form a Venn diagram but actually just two perfectly overlapping circles."

She could only smile at that. "Well, the good news is that now that I'm here, there's nothing for me to do but help you prepare for your wedding. And as long as no one expects us to turn it into a double wedding, with me marrying some surprise stranger I only meet at the end of the aisle, then any aversion I feel to the idea of marriage is completely moot. After all, I'm not against other people getting married." She shrugged. "I'm just not convinced it's for me. But I'm here—I came all this way—to get you married, Celia. Just don't try to sell me the idea of a double wedding and there's literally nothing I won't do to make your big day everything you want it to be."

Celia narrowed her eyes at her friend. "You mean that?"

Eve nodded. "Of course I do. I'm not sure which part you mean, since I did say a lot of things just then." She lifted her shoulders. "But I meant it all, so I stand by my original response."

"Well then." Celia carefully scooped a protesting Badem off her lap and transferred her to the empty cushion between them on the couch before getting to her feet. "Let's go!"

Seven

Luna Düğün Salonu was a large building, located just a short walk from Enes and Celia's apartment. It was as if every hotel conference room she had ever been in had been taken out of context and turned into its own freestanding building, and then the classiness had been dialed up to eleven. There were marble columns around the doors and statues in the parking lot, and Eve could only imagine what awaited inside.

"So this place is only for weddings?" Eve asked as they approached the building. "Do you rent out the whole building?"

"This one is big enough that they can have a couple of events at the same time," Celia explained as they entered. "And I really think it is just weddings they have here. I mean, you could rent the space for, say, a circumcision ceremony or something—"

"I'm sorry, a what?" Eve asked, stopping in her tracks.

Celia smiled. "It's like a coming-of-age celebration for the boys. I saw some photos from when Enes had his, and he was dressed up like a little prince. Kind of adorable, even if the concept is pretty unfamiliar for those of us outside the culture." She nodded towards the door and the two of them went inside. "But anyway, like I was saying, it's right there in the name, Düğün Salonu. It means 'wedding salon,' so it might be a bit confusing if you were having some sort of different celebration or ceremony here."

"Right." Eve nodded. "I'm still stuck on circumcision, but I promise I'll move on, eventually. They aren't, like, performing the actual operation, are they? I feel like, if I were the boy coming of age, that's the last thing I would want to have publicly celebrated."

"They are not," said Celia, with a small shake of her head. Before she could say anything further, though, a black and white shape flew past them, making it through the door just before it swung closed.

"What the heck?" Eve asked, her eyes tracking the blur. "What was that? A tiny ghost? A large bird?"

Celia chuckled. "Both great guesses, but I believe it was a cat." She nodded in the direction where the blur had disappeared. "Let's see if we can find it. I can't imagine the owners of this place would want to have a cat stuck inside overnight."

As they followed the cat further inside, they found themselves walking down a long hallway. There was the faint sound of music, which got louder as they continued on their way, until it reached peak volume when a door opened off the hallway. A quick glance inside told Eve there was a wedding happening in there, and she froze in her tracks, eyes darting to Celia.

"It's a wedding," she hissed. "Do you think the cat went in there?"

Celia shook her head. "Do you hear how loud that music is? I barely even want to go in there, and I'm not a cat. I'm sure it's just looking for food or something." She nodded towards the hallway. "There's probably a kitchen or something back this way, and we just might catch it in the act of stealing its dinner."

Celia's phone buzzed in her hand, and she glanced down on it, wincing at what was on the screen. "Shoot," she said, jerking her head back in the direction they had come from. "That's Jasmine. She just got here, and she doesn't have a lot of time. I need to go meet her and look at the her plan." She gave Eve an apologetic smile. "Do you think you can handle this?"

Even though Eve desperately wanted to say, "No, I can't. I'm coming with you," and leave the whole cat fiasco to someone else to sort out, she found herself nodding. "Yeah, it's no problem at all." She bit her lip. "But if your meeting ends and I still haven't come back, then maybe come help me, okay? I mean, if one of us is the cat whisperer, it's definitely you. And if one of us is apt to get lured into a walk-in freezer by a cat and then locked in there, it's definitely me."

"Fair enough." Celia nodded. "I promise I won't leave without you, and I'll check every locked door to find you if I have to."

With resignation, Eve set off in search of the cat, glancing over her shoulder just once to confirm that Celia must have jogged to her meeting, as she was already out of sight.

"Okay then," she said out loud. "Where the heck are you?"

She caught a glimpse of a familiar monochromatic blur disappearing around a corner up ahead, and she picked up her pace into a jog to try to catch the cat before it was out of sight again. "Stay right there, you little stinker," she hissed, flying around the corner and crouching as if she expected to find the cat right in that spot, just sitting there and waiting to be grabbed.

Alas, it was not the cat that she met first. Just as she crouched down, she became aware of a hulking figure approaching from the opposite direction, something vaguely man-shaped, though it had a shiny contraption slung around its neck. As she ducked, the man—*for what else would be man-shaped but an actual man?* she wondered—turned his head to look at something and the two of them collided.

Because of Eve's low position and their opposing inertias, the collision that happened when their bodies met was something that would have made the NFL proud. She realized only when the man's feet had both left the ground that the contraption around his neck was an expensive-looking camera, and as she rose to her feet in slow motion, she watched him twist his body to shield the device from impact before he crashed back to the ground.

She rushed over to him then, to where he was lying on his back, a pained expression already crossing his face. "Oh my gosh," she cried, reaching her hands out to examine him but then stopping herself before she made contact. "Are you okay? Are you hurt?" Her eyes, which had been combing his body for obvious signs of injury, found his face then and she gulped as she took him in. *Did I just maim a model? Shit.* "Do you speak English?" she asked, realizing that her other questions would have been pointless if he did not answer this one in the affirmative.

He nodded and groaned as he reached up a hand to feel the back of his head. "I do speak English, and I believe I am okay." He got himself up to a seat and then looked at her with a quizzical expression. "But I do need to ask you if you are okay. I'm not sure where you're from, but here in Turkey, we generally don't tackle strangers in hallways." He winced as he got to his feet, and a part of her longed to put her hands on his shoulders, to stop him, to warn him that he might be hurt and that he should stay put until she could get a doctor to come look at him. *To keep him right here with me a little longer*, a voice in the back of her head said, confusing her. "Actually," he said, "I don't know of any culture where tackling strangers is socially acceptable. It seems more like something Mr. Bean would do for some ridiculous misunderstanding than something that would happen between two real people."

"I'm so sorry," she said, the words tumbling out. "I was trying to catch a cat, I swear. I don't normally sneak around weddings dressed like this, tackling people." She gestured down to her sweatsuit, his eyes tracking her hands.

"Right." He nodded. "A cat, you say?" He pointed over her shoulder. "It wouldn't happen to be that guy, would it?"

She moved her eyes, following the length of his finger and then tracking where it was pointing. Sure enough, sitting in the base of a large potted plant, was a cat. It must have been the same blur of motion she had seen before, because as she saw now it was a tuxedo cat, mostly black, but with a streak of white down the front of his body, white features on his face, and white socks at the end of each leg. "That's him!" she cried, about to set off in the direction of the cat.

"Wait." The man dropped a hand on her forearm, shaking his head. "Unless you want a repeat of what just happened between us, don't chase him." He tilted his head back in the direction she had come from. "Come with me."

As they began to walk away from the cat, Eve felt her brow crease with concern. "Um, why are we walking *away* from the source of our worries? It's a cat. He's not going to follow us."

The man looked down at her then, his dark eyes probing hers, giving her the feeling that he was seeing deeply, far too deeply for your usual comfort level. "Are you sure?" he asked, and she nodded slowly in response, swallowing an unfamiliar feeling but dismayed to feel how dry her mouth was.

"I think so," she said, "but I'm not a cat behavior expert."

He chuckled at that, before reaching into his pocket and pulling out a small packet, which he shook. "Lucky for you, then, that I am."

He raised his eyebrows before dropping his gaze meaningfully down to their feet, and when Eve looked down, she was shocked to see the cat circling his legs.

"What in the—?" She asked, reaching for his arm to pull the packet closer and study it. "What is this? Catnip?"

"Oh, it's even better than that." He slipped the pouch open in one quick movement and poured the contents onto his palm. "Treats! I carry them with me in case I see a photo opportunity just waiting to happen." He dropped down to give the cat one of the treats, the small brown square vanishing in one movement of its jaw, before coming back to his full height, continuing to walk towards the door. "Let's use the rest of these treats to take this guy outside before he crashes the wedding or you crash into one of the guests."

Eve winced as she jogged to keep up with him. "I really am sorry about that. Are you okay?" Her mouth dropped in horror. "Is your camera okay? I can—"

He lifted one hand to cut her off, giving her a devastating smile in the process. "It would take more than one tackle—a good, solid tackle, I'll give you that much—to bring me or my camera down." He lifted the camera, rotating it in his hand as he studied it from all angles. "It looks fine to me, but I'll take some pictures when we're outside to make sure nothing got rattled inside." He smiled at her. "I shielded it with my body."

"I saw that." She winced again. "It was an impressive move."

He nodded. "I think we both proved that we could have had great careers as professional athletes if we hadn't found our true callings as photographer and..." He studied her, looking for some clue of her profession. "Well, I assume you aren't a professional wedding crasher or cat wrangler, but I could be wrong."

"I don't think wedding crashing is actually something you can get paid to do," she said, "and if I were a professional cat wrangler, then surely my performance on that front today would be poor enough to suggest I'm not actually very good at it. No, actually I'm a software developer." She held up a hand before he could speak. "And that has nothing to do with why I'm here today."

The man nodded as he held the door open for her and for the cat, both of them slipping outside and one of them looking expectantly up at his handsome face for some more of those tasty treats. As the cat started to munch, the man looked at Eve as if he were trying to figure it out.

"Are you here to arrange your wedding, then?" A look of something similar to horror crossed his face before his next words tumbled out. "Am I your photographer? Have we already met?"

She threw her head back and laughed out loud. "My gosh, wouldn't that be the worst? Not only have we already met and my hunky fiancé has already paid a hefty deposit for your services at our wedding, but now you don't even remember it and we just smashed our bodies into each other in an entirely unsexy but also entirely unprofessional manner." She shook her head then, putting him out of his misery. "No, we haven't met and I'm not getting married. I'm here to help my friend get ready for her wedding."

Relief washed over the man's face as he nodded. "That's good. You seemed familiar somehow, and it is definitely not a good look for the guy who's supposed to be so good with faces to not remember meeting the bride. So I'm glad it's not your wedding." His cheeks had turned ever so slightly pink, and was it her imagination, or was he avoiding meeting her gaze?

"I'm glad it's not my wedding, too," said Eve. "Not only because I'm sure my best friend would never speak to me again if I married her fiancé out from underneath her, but also because there's probably some rule about brides not tackling handsome strangers before the wedding."

He chuckled softly as he watched the cat eat its last few treats. "I'm Umut, by the way," he said, holding out his hand for her to shake.

"Eve," she said, as she shook it. "It's nice to meet you. Sorry again for tackling you."

It was at that precise moment, just as those words had left her mouth, that the door of Luna Düğün Salonu opened and Celia came out with another woman, horrified looks on both of their faces.

"Eve…" Celia began, with hesitation in her voice. "Why did you tackle my photographer?" Her eyes darted from Eve to Umut as if she could read the situation between them, retrace the steps that had brought them from where she had left Eve alone in the hallway to where she was finding the two of them together now. As she glanced down at the cat, she laughed. "Ah," she said. "I think I see what happened here."

Eve looked at her askance. "You do? Because I'll be shocked if you can get it right." She crossed her arms over her chest, nodding at her friend, who was grinning at her like she knew a secret.

"Well, if I had to guess, I'd say this little gentleman here—" She nodded at the cat. "—organized a meet-cute of sorts for the two of you." She pointed at Eve. "You were chasing him down the hallway, and you were so focused on catching him that you didn't see Umut—" She pointed at him then. "—and the two of you crashed into each other." She shook her head. "It'll be a great story to tell the grandkids, but I hope neither of you got hurt. And that your camera is okay, Umut. Is your camera okay?"

Umut nodded at her, but he looked stunned into silence. Eve, for her part, was still trying to decipher her friend's words. Sure, she had more or less figured out exactly what had transpired in her absence...but was she really implying now that this cat was some kind of matchmaker?

The woman next to Celia, no doubt sensing the awkwardness both Eve and Umut were feeling, as well as Celia's apparent obliviousness to it, stepped forward then.

"Hi." She held out her hand to Eve, who shook it automatically. "I'm Jasmine, and I'm helping out with the food for the wedding reception. You must be Eve, and it's really nice to meet you. I'd tell you to ignore Celia since she's clearly got nothing but love and weddings on the brain, but you know her better than I do." She turned and smiled at Umut then. "Nice to see you too, Umut." Looking at them both, she jerked her head toward the door. "Should we all go inside and check out the space, then? I guess it's nothing new for Umut, but Eve, we could use some input on where to set up the dessert tables."

Umut reached into his pocket for a few more treats for the cat, the four humans slipping quickly through the door while the small creature dug in.

"I think I'm going to miss that little guy," Eve said to Umut as she glanced back out the door. The smile he gave her in response was difficult to read, but she didn't dwell on it, focusing her attention on Celia and Jasmine, the grand room they were entering, and the grand problem of pastry arrangement.

Eight

As soon as they stepped back into the lowering sun outside the wedding salon, the cryptic smile Umut had given her made sense.

"Ah." Eve nodded as she studied the newly awakened cat who was stretching every muscle in his body, right down to his individual toe beans, and meowing up at them as if they were sailors returning from a trip around the world. "So it turns out I didn't need to miss you, did I?" She crouched down to scratch the cat behind the ears, glancing up at Umut, who was smiling down at her.

"I think he works here," he said. "He's around a lot, anyway."

"That makes sense given his uniform," she replied. "Where else would he work, dressed in a tuxedo like that?"

Celia and Jasmine had hung back, still making some decisions about flavors of cakes and the appropriate number of servings, and Eve got back to her feet, standing next to Umut as the cat began to wind its way through their legs.

"He's awfully cute," she said. "I'd take him home if I had a home to take him to. I'm not sure how Celia and

Enes's cat would feel if I brought a strange animal into the house."

Umut studied her with narrowed eyes. "Is this a guilt trip to get me to take him home?" He reached up to rub the back of his neck. "Because I had actually been thinking of that, but now that you suggested it, I don't want you to think I'm doing your every bidding just an hour after we met."

She snorted. "I would never think that. And no, I wasn't trying to manipulate you into adopting a cat." She nodded towards the street. "Just feeling concerned about this little guy out here with a bustling street right over there. It's not necessarily a safe world out there for a little cat on his own."

He nodded. "It certainly isn't." He looked down at the cat then, speaking directly to him. "What do you say, sir? I don't want to force anything on you, so...if you want to come home with me, just...well, come home with me, okay?"

I'll come home with you. The thought popped into Eve's mind completely unbidden, slipping in so naturally and so unexpectedly that she nearly shrieked at the contents of her own mind. Instead, she pulled her phone out of her pocket and spent the next few moments deleting junk emails while waiting for Celia and Jasmine to return and pointedly not talking to Umut.

When the women rejoined them, all four of them set off walking together, and as if he had listened to Umut's words, the cat tagged along with them. He walked between Umut and Eve, glancing up at each of them in turn as if to check that they were still right where he expected them to be.

The four of them—four humans, that is, along with their feline companion—walked together for a couple of blocks, stopping at a corner.

"I'm this way," said Umut, jerking his thumb to the left.

"And we are all that way," said Celia, pointing to the right. "Are you heading home, Jas?"

Jasmine shook her head, nodding straight ahead. "I should go to the cafe, see if I'm needed there."

They all said their goodbyes then, and as Eve and Celia began walking away, a plaintive howl came from near Umut's feet. As she turned to look, he crouched down to scoop up the cat. While the cat hadn't followed Eve, it had been kneading its paws onto the sidewalk, meowing in a distressed tone just before Umut had picked it up. The meows had softened somewhat now that the animal was safe in Umut's arms, but it wasn't until Eve began walking back towards the two of them that the cat visibly relaxed, his cries replaced by purrs.

Celia had followed her friend, a puzzled look on her face as Eve reached out to stroke the cat's head, painfully aware of how close her hand was to Umut's chest.

"What's going on with you?" Celia asked, reaching to the cat, who leaned forward to rub his cheek against her hand. "Aren't you going to let us go home? Eve is staying with me, Mister, and you can't have her."

Eve felt her cheeks heat, panic that her friend was about to start sharing her theories about matchmaking cats again and, in an effort to keep that from happening, said the first thing that came to her mind.

"I can walk with you. Just to help him settle in, I mean. If you stand here on the street corner with a howling cat, someone is going to call the police."

Celia raised an eyebrow, but Umut only chuckled. "If someone called the police in Istanbul every time a cat yowled, the crime would be out of control in this city." He smiled at her then. "You are, of course, welcome to join us, but please don't feel obligated."

Eve looked at Celia, asking her friend with her eyes if this was a terrible idea. She had only met Umut today, after all, and even though she believed herself to be a good judge of character, it wasn't exactly a normal behavior for her to invite herself to a strange man's home.

Celia only smiled. "Could you walk Eve home later, Umut? I doubt she knows her way around the neighborhood, and I wouldn't want her to get lost. You could stay for dinner, too. I know Enes would love to spend some quality time with his favorite cousin."

Ah. Eve gave her friend the slightest of nods. *They're cousins. So that's why you trust him so much. And also probably why you're so interested in setting the two of us up.*

"Does that sound good to you, Eve?" asked Umut, and she felt two sets of eyes on her. Three sets, in fact, as the cat was studying her too.

"Yeah, great." She nodded, swallowing against a sudden feeling of dryness in her throat. She turned to look at Celia. "I'm sure we won't be long. I mean, obviously I don't know where Umut lives or even where you live, but what I'm saying is that I'm not planning to stay out for a super long time. I want to spend time with you, after all. That's what I'm here for."

Celia placed her hand on Eve's forearm. "And you've got almost two weeks to do exactly that." She nodded towards Umut and the cat. "Don't forget, I'm uniquely qualified on matters of cat-related serendipity. It would be incredibly hypocritical of me to insist you ignore the signs and meows when I'm literally about to get married as a result of my own feline matchmaker."

"Right." Eve spoke through gritted teeth, dropping the volume of her voice so that Umut wouldn't hear. "I guess I couldn't have dared to hope that you wouldn't have said something like that right where he can hear you, but, hey. What do I know?"

Celia only shook her head. "Umut?" she called, lifting her chin in his direction. "Am I making you uncomfortable with all of my talk of matchmaking? Does it feel like I'm putting pressure on you?"

He shook his head. "Not at all. I know your story, so I know you and Enes are both experts on the subject." He looked at Eve then, giving her a reassuring smile. "I think it's just her way of saying that she likes both of us and wouldn't mind if we also liked each other. But I don't think she's trying to pressure us into anything."

"No?" Eve raised an eyebrow. "Because I had heard that when your best friend gets married, it's very common for her to start trying to fix you up with every other single person she knows. Like married people are allergic to having single friends and must see every one of us paired off."

"Hey!" Celia protested, crossing her arms over her chest. "I have dropped two very casual comments about one good man. That hardly qualifies as trying to pair you off with every single person I know."

"That's true," said Eve, "but to be fair, Umut is the first single person I've met in Istanbul. And it hasn't even been a day since I arrived."

Umut turned his head so quickly to look at her she experienced secondhand dizziness just observing the movement. "You arrived today?" When she nodded, he only shook his head. "You must be exhausted." He hefted the cat in his arms, earning one small meow of protest in the process. "You don't have to come with us, not today. I'm sure I can get this guy home and settled with a minimum of complaints, and you can come visit him some other day if you'd like to."

Eve shook her head, surprised at how disappointed she felt at imagining cutting her time with Umut short. "No, it's really okay. Walking is good for me, and it sounds like a fun project. I've never gotten to see a cat settle into a new house, and I don't want to miss it."

He nodded, a smile spreading across his face. "Great. Then Celia, we'll see you later. Maybe in about an hour?"

Eve waved at her friend, setting off next to Umut, who was still cradling the cat in his arms.

Nine

They hadn't walked long before the cat reached out a paw towards Eve, a claw getting snagged on her bracelet.

"Hey." She smiled as she pulled her hand back after freeing it from the cat's sharp talon. "Did you need something?"

"Do you want to hold him?" Umut asked, holding out the cat, which she readily folded into her arms. "It isn't far."

She tucked the cat's head under her chin, feeling warmed from within as his purring body vibrated against her torso. At a moment like that, it was easy to believe that a cat's purrs could heal. She took the fact that this cat had chosen her and was now so happy to be in her arms that he was purring loudly enough she could barely carry on a conversation with Umut as the ultimate compliment. She might not be a perfect person, but she had the approval of this cat, and at the moment, it was hard to imagine needing anything else.

"Have you thought about what to name him?" she asked Umut, one hand tucking the cat close as her other hand scratched behind his ears.

"I was going to ask for a suggestion, actually," he said. "I've been trying to think of something clever but that I won't get tired of saying, and I haven't had any great ideas yet."

"Hmm." She pulled her head back slightly to look down at the animal, seeing if any inspiration was waiting to leap off of him. "Maybe something about the fact that he's such a fancy boy in his snazzy tuxedo. What do you call a tuxedo cat in Turkish, anyway?"

Umut chuckled. "He's called a *smokin kedisi*, which probably sounds a bit funny in English. But as an ex-smoker myself—yes, despite my wholesome appearance I was young and rebellious once—I'm not so inclined to name my cat something that implies he's smoking cigars with all the other fancy boys."

"Definitely not." She wrinkled her nose. "What about Orca?"

He paused with his mouth agape, then stopped walking and turned to look at the cat. He reached out a hand, lifting the whiskered chin so that the two of them were looking into each other's eyes. "Are you an Orca? Do you like that name?" He studied the cat a moment longer, then nodded and took his hand back, starting off down the street once again.

"That settles it. Orca it is."

"Really?" She took one jogging step to catch up with him, energized as he had clearly been by the successful naming of his new cat. "He's your cat. You don't have to give him a name I suggest, just because you're being polite." She sniffed then. "Of course, when I leave from all of your lives in a couple weeks, you can call him whatever you want and I will never know. I imagine it wouldn't be too hard to swear Enes and Celia to secrecy."

If there was a part of her that was already feeling possessive, not just of the cat but of the man as well, then she really didn't know what to do with it. She had spoken the truth—it wasn't as if she had any long-term plans as far as Umut, Orca, or Istanbul were concerned, so she hardly had the right to make any claims on what the cat should be called or who Umut should share him with.

He only narrowed his eyes at her, though. "First of all, Orca is an objectively excellent name, and I won't hear any objection to it. And second of all, if you think I'm going to let my cousin and his new wife lie to you after you waltz out of their life…" A devilish glint flashed in his eye. "And third of all, if you think I'm going to just let you waltz—"

She held up a hand to stop him, even though her heart was racing to hear how he would end that sentence. God help her, she knew he was joking, and yet thanks to her exhaustion and disorientation, she was about to take him seriously. If she let him finish that sentence, there was a good chance she might hold him to whatever threat he made. She was going to need to sleep for at least sixteen hours to get her head on straight if she was thinking this rashly.

"Are we almost to your apartment?" she asked, hefting the cat in her arms. "Orca is cute, but he's a little squirmy and I'm sure we would both like to have him be free from my arms."

"It's that one right there." Umut pointed at a building across the street, then glanced back and forth for a break in traffic before sliding his hand around Eve's elbow and guiding her seamlessly across the road.

She smiled at him once they had made it to the other side. "Thanks," she said. "I was tempted to tell you that I can cross a street by myself, but I realized halfway across that it was actually nice to have someone else take responsibility for my safety." She gestured back towards the street. "Especially in an unfamiliar city where I'm not entirely sure if the cars are going to stop or even slow down before they hit me."

"An understandable concern." He nodded. "I'm happy to help. Plus, I would feel responsible if anything happened to you, especially if it happened because the little troublemaker in your arms started wiggling or scratched you or something equally life-threatening."

They had arrived at Umut's building, and he opened the gate, holding it open for Eve and Orca. She shook her head when he raised an eyebrow in a silent offer to take the cat from her hands, his outstretched hands clearly communicating his intentions. Not only did she not know what she would do with her hands if the squirming cat were no longer in them, but she had a strong suspicion that once they were inside and she relinquished the animal, he would be enjoying his newfound freedom and cat cuddles would be a rare commodity.

Umut's apartment was on the second floor, and Eve took a sharp intake of breath as they stepped inside. She didn't know what she had expected from this man she had barely known long enough to form an impression, but it wasn't this. Not only was the apartment just the right combination of tidy and lived in, but the wall was covered in beautiful artwork, black and white photographs of rushing water and ornate flowers, portraits of laughing families interspersed among them.

Realization dawned on her as she felt Umut studying her reaction. "Are these...yours?" she asked, nodding towards the photographs. "Did you take these pictures?"

He nodded, reaching again for the cat, who she handed over this time. "Do you like them?" he asked, before wincing. "Sorry. That's an awkward question. I'm not hunting for praise or needing constant validation. I just...is this a style of photography you enjoy? Or is your apartment decorated in a different way?"

The last thing she would do in that moment was admit there wasn't even a print she had bought at Target adorning the walls of her St. Louis apartment. For someone who clearly had an eye for beauty, that was bound to be the ultimate sin. "It's beautiful," she said at last, stopping herself from reaching out to touch a photograph of an older woman with the warmest smile and kindest eyes, someone who looked vaguely familiar and yet who Eve was sure she had never met—she would remember her if she had.

"Is this Badem?" she asked, whirling to face Umut as she trailed along the gallery wall before stopping at a picture of a familiar tabby.

He nodded, holding up Orca to show him the picture as well. "That's your cousin, Orca. I'll take you to meet her dad soon, and once we have you squared away with your vet checkup, maybe we can arrange a playdate for the two of you."

Eve smiled at the thought of the two cats on a playdate. "How does that work? They play together? Or do they just hiss at each other for about ten minutes and then take a nap?"

"We'll see, I guess." Umut shrugged. "But I'd imagine they'll get along quite well, considering how social they both are."

There was something about the thought of Umut and Orca having regular play dates with Celia, Enes, and Badem that wasn't sitting quite right in Eve's stomach. Was it...jealousy? Surely she wasn't curdling from the inside out over the thought of two cats batting around a catnip mouse with each other.

Ahh, but Enes and Celia will be spending time with Umut at the same time, though I'm sure they do that already. After all, who cared if she was invited along to their extended family gatherings? Enes probably had plenty of cousins in the city, and she wasn't bothered by not getting to know any of them.

It's possible there's something different about Umut, you know, an obnoxious voice in the back of her mind informed her. *It might not even be about Enes's distant relations at all, but simply about this one.* Shaking it off, she pointed to the picture of the vaguely familiar woman on the wall.

"Who is this, and why do I feel like I know her?"

Umut smiled, his eyes crinkling at the corners. "That is Meryem Teyze, Enes's mother. My aunt. Though she is like a mother to me, too."

Eve raised an eyebrow, but before she could ask her question, he continued.

"My own mother passed away. Five years ago now. Meryem Teyze has always been a favorite, but she has especially taken care of me since then. You probably recognize her because there is so much of her in her son."

"I'm so sorry to hear about your mom. That must have been hard."

"Thank you. It was, but it's better with the support of the rest of the family."

Eve nodded, not sure what to say next. Umut, whether inspired by the new awkwardness between them or a genuine need, slapped his hands on his upper thighs and looked at her expectantly.

"Would you mind keeping an eye on Orca while I run out and get a litter box? I thought I still had one here in the house somewhere, but then I remembered I gave it to Jasmine when she was taking donations for the cafe. I'd ask you to come with me, but I think it's too soon to trust Orca here on his own—"

"Especially without a litter box," Eve cut in. "And it's fine. I'm happy to keep an eye on him. You...uh...won't be gone long?" She chuckled nervously. "It's just that if you were to leave me here and never come back, I'd be sort of stranded. At least until Enes and Celia realize I haven't come home yet and come looking for me."

He smiled at her. "That sounds like a cruel joke, and I promise I had nothing of the sort in mind. It's just a couple of blocks to the pet store, and I'll be back as quickly as I can be." He patted his pocket then, nodding when he confirmed his wallet was there. "In fact, the sooner I leave, the sooner I'll be back. Do you need anything before I go? A drink, a snack?" When she shook her head, he gave a quick nod. "If you change your mind, then just help yourself. Make yourself at home, I mean. I've got nothing to hide, so feel free to have a little snoop around."

And before she could protest that she was not, in fact, interested in poking around in his medicine cabinet or kitchen junk drawer, Umut was gone.

"Well then." She looked down at Orca, who was sitting at her feet and looking up at her face with expectation. "Looks like it's just us cool cats, then. What kind of trouble should we get into?"

When Orca didn't offer any suggestions, Eve returned to the photographs, perusing them more slowly this time. She took in the details, the intentional composition, the movement. Every one of them made her appreciate Umut's eye at a new level, putting her in real danger of either developing an inferiority complex around his talent or falling promptly in love with him because of it.

She was studying the family photos again when there was a knock at the door. She started at the sound, pulled out of her reverie by the sharpness of it.

"Umut?" she called as she began walking towards the door. "Is that you?" She stopped before she reached the door. Of course it wasn't him. He would have taken his key with him, wouldn't he? He had shown her a spare key he kept in the kitchen, had told her he didn't want to leave her stranded inside and lock the door behind him because it felt too much like a gothic novel, but she was quite sure he had brought a key with him.

"Umut!" A stern voice called from the other side of the door, only a name recognizable to Eve along with a string of rapid-fire Turkish.

She ventured closer to the door, tiptoeing so that she wouldn't be detected as she peeked through the peephole.

When she saw the figure on the other side, she threw the door open so quickly that the petite woman on the other side jumped back, one hand flying to her sternum.

"You're Enes's mom!" Eve cried, reaching her arms out to steady the older woman and then to pull her into the apartment. "I was just looking at a photo of you and thinking of how much I wanted to meet you. Did I make this happen with my brain?" She wrinkled her forehead, a nervous chuckle escaping. "Do you speak English, and did I scare you too much? I'm so sorry. I'm Eve. I'm Celia's friend from back home and—"

"I know who you are." Enes's mother gave her a gentle push back as she slipped off her shoes and stepped into Umut's apartment, handing a pot to Eve. "And of course I speak English. You know that's how I met Celia, when I was helping my son at his clinic." She narrowed her eyes at Eve then. "And I wanted to meet you too, but I can't for the life of me figure out what you're doing here at Umut's apartment. And where is he? Why is he sending you to answer the door?" She waved a hand at Eve. "I can't keep up with you kids. You probably met already on the Instabook or Facegram or whatever it's called. Everyone will laugh at old Meryem, at how out of date she is with all the technology. Everyone meets on the internet these days, you know."

"Oh?" Eve tipped her head towards the kitchen. "Why don't we go sit down, maybe have some tea?" She lifted the pot Meryem had handed her. "I should put this in the kitchen, I think."

Meryem nodded. "It needs to finish cooking. If you put it on the stove on low, you can eat it in half an hour."

"Oh, actually maybe I should put it in the fridge then for Umut to eat tomorrow. We were going to have dinner with Enes and Celia tonight." And then, because her statement struck her as rude, she hurried to invite Enes's mother along. "You should come too, of course. I'm sure you would be more than welcome."

Meryem frowned. "Of course I would be welcome, but even I know that a guest needs at least two days to recover before you start rushing them all over town and introducing them to everyone." She sat down on the couch as Eve began to boil some water for tea, checking surreptitiously in the cabinets for the tea bags she was sure Umut must have on hand.

But Enes's mother only patted the couch next to her. "Come sit with me. Humor me for a moment." As Eve was making her way over to join her, Orca appeared, reemerging from behind the couch where he had hidden at the first knock on the door. "Oh!" Meryem cried, leaning forward to get a better look at him and reaching out to grab him before he could disappear again. "And who is this?" Her eyes narrowed at Eve. "Is this your cat? Is he jet lagged, too?"

Eve chuckled as she shook her head. "No, he's actually Umut's new cat. We all just met, actually, at the wedding salon."

Meryem nodded slowly, as if she were still processing Eve's words. "So what you're saying is that it may have happened quickly, but it was love at first sight?" She had been scratching Orca's chin, winning him over immediately judging by the sound of his purrs, but she looked up directly into Eve's eyes then. "For all three of you, I mean. Anyone can think a cat is cute at first sight, but you can't deny there were some sparks between you and Umut."

"I—uh. I mean," Eve sputtered. "No, it isn't like that. I'm just here for the wedding, and even though Celia and Enes are practically the poster children for Istanbul cats' matchmaking abilities, that isn't what's happening here."

Meryem looked skeptical as she raised an eyebrow at Eve. "You sound awfully sure of yourself for someone who clearly doesn't know a meet-cute when she experiences one." She leaned forward then. "Did I use that right, meet-cute? Celia taught me the phrase when I was preparing a speech for the wedding, and I've never used it out of that context."

"Oh, you got it exactly right. I mean, I'm not willing to agree with you that a meet-cute is what happened between me and Umut, but I'm fully confident that the word describes what you believe happened."

Meryem threw back her head and laughed so loudly that Orca jumped off her lap and disappeared behind the couch again. "Are you a lawyer?" she asked, narrowing her eyes. "Because that sounds like the way someone who plays with words for a living would say."

"Not a lawyer." Eve shook her head. "But I do play with language and logic." Then, when Meryem looked at her with an expectant tilt of her head, she continued. "I'm a computer programmer."

Meryem waved a dismissive hand. "If you say so, honey. But tell me, how *did* you and Umut meet?"

Ten

Eve had time to finish the story of how she had met Umut by the time he returned from his hunting and gathering. The story had taken longer than it should have because Meryem had been full of questions—she needed to know every detail—and because the meaningful glances she gave Eve every other sentence required at least a moment of silence each. It was clear she was holding back, saving her final verdict for the end of the story, at which time Eve expected to hear a full-length movie monologue.

And so it was with no sadness at all that she heard the sound of Umut's key in the lock and relaxed further back into the couch. Girl talk was over. The time for grilling Eve was over. Umut could hold his own, she was sure, considering that Meryem was like a mother to him. All these factors combined meant she was off the hook.

But, of course, it was actually possible for a person to be wrong about everything.

As soon as Umut was inside, before they could even see him, he was calling out. "Eve? Is everything okay? I got all your stuff, Orca! Yes, I sure did! Check it out, sniff the bags."

That was how Eve realized Orca had snuck out from his hiding spot and into the hall.

"We're in here!" she called, her voice feeling strained in her throat.

"We?" Umut asked, but as he entered the room, his confusion was replaced with laughter. "Meryem Teyze! You're here, and you met my guest, I see. Both of them!"

Now it was his turn to receive a dismissive wave from Meryem. "What do you mean, guest? That cat lives with you now, and so will this woman soon if I have anything to say about it!" She gestured towards Eve. "Tell her, Umut, because she won't listen to me. Tell her that the two of you meeting today was no mere coincidence, that it's surely fate." Her eyes widened suddenly, and she jumped to her feet. "I know! I should make Turkish coffee." She leaned towards Umut and lowered her voice, but not so much that Eve couldn't hear. "Then I can read her fortune and she'll believe me!"

There was nothing for Eve to do but pretend she hadn't heard and hope the moment passed or that, in whatever unspoken communication was passing between them, Umut was forbidding his aunt from continuing her matchmaking/fortune-telling torment. The discussion seemed to end as Meryem made her way to the kitchen and the sound of running water and then a kettle being switched on reached Eve's ears.

She got up and joined Orca where he was investigating the purchases Umut had brought home. "What have we here?" she said, looking over his shoulder into a bag that clearly smelled fascinating.

"That's right," said Umut as he came to join them. "I was halfway to the pet store when I remembered that Enes sells all of this stuff at his vet practice and I'd be a fool to get it anywhere else."

"But he isn't there!" called Meryem from the kitchen. "And neither am I, as you can see."

"Right." Umut nodded. "It would have been good if I had realized that before I walked there, but no harm. I ended up back at the pet store, just as I had originally planned, and I may have done a few impulse buys." He reached into the bag and pulled out a pouch of treats and a battery-powered mouse. "I just couldn't resist!"

Umut flipped a switch on the bottom of the mouse toy, then set it on the floor where it began to move around in erratic patterns and rhythms. Orca perked up immediately, crouching as his eyes tracked its movement, his rear end shaking ever so subtly just before he pounced on the toy and fell over, bunny kicking it ferociously.

Eve couldn't help but laugh. While she would be horrified if Orca were doing the same thing with a real mouse, there was something about the way he played with his toy that leaned much further towards the "adorable" end of the kitty spectrum rather than the "homicidal maniac" end.

"He's the cutest," she said, looking up from the cat to find Umut's eyes already on her, an unknown Something passing over his expression as if he had just answered a particularly puzzling question. "Don't tell Badem I said that, though. And kudos to you for making the clear right decision today in taking this little guy home."

"Oh, well, I mean…" He reached over and rubbed Orca's belly, which earned him some playful nibbles, before the cat jumped to his feet and took off after the mouse again. "I owe him a debt of gratitude for facilitating our introduction, so I figure committing to take care of him for the rest of his life is the least I could do." He winked at her then, before getting to his feet and heading into the kitchen to help his aunt, the whole thing happening too quickly for her to decide if he was kidding or serious.

As the three of them had shared cups of tea and conversation, Umut and Meryem were all too ready to offer suggestions for places Eve should see while in Istanbul and things she should do. Umut offered to accompany her to nearly all of them, something she couldn't let herself overthink. When the last of the tea was gone, it was time to make the short walk to Enes and Celia's apartment.

Umut made sure everything was set up for Orca, that there was a minimum of trouble he could get himself into while they were gone, while Eve helped Meryem clean up the dishes. Then, they walked together, and it was then that Eve learned just how close Meryem lived to her son and Celia.

"Well, you have to join us then…right?" She looked at Umut with expectation. "I mean, it hardly seems right for her to be so close and not come spend the evening with us."

Meryem put a hand on Eve's arm and shook her head. "You're very sweet, dear, but I have too many things calling me home right now. A cake in the oven, in fact!" She chuckled then. "Oh, don't look so surprised. I left my husband with strict instructions on when and in what condition to take it out of the oven. I have no plans to burn down my home by lingering over a cup of tea with you."

Umut smiled down at the two of them. "Rest assured, this won't be the last you see of Meryem Teyze, Eve."

"Oh indeed!" Meryem crowed. "By the end of your visit, you'll be trying to avoid me, not inviting me to join!"

"I highly doubt that." Eve shook her head. Meryem had the same inviting air as all of Eve's favorite people back home, the cousin she stayed up late gossiping with at every family gathering, the uncle she sought out every time he came back into town so that the two of them could geek out about computers, something the rest of the family never understood. She felt like an old friend and a brand new acquaintance who was the coolest person she had ever met, and at the same time like the sort of person you could just share comfortable silence with and never tire of being around.

But of course, all of that was too much to tell Meryem now, so a heartfelt smile would have to suffice. She felt a frown crease her forehead as she realized those same words could be used to describe how she felt around Umut, too.

That has to be the jet lag talking, she thought. *It's clearly having the same effect as drinking a bottle of red on an empty stomach—suddenly I love everyone and want them to be my best friend.* She shuddered at the thought, at the memory of younger and more impulsive days when an entire bottle of wine had seemed like a good idea. These days, she was much more of a "single glass before dinner" kind of gal.

And so she buttoned her lips. If she was still this en-thralled with Meryem and Umut in a few days, she could consider saying something to them then. But in the meantime, it was best she keep her uninhibited adorations to herself.

In a very short time they had arrived at Enes and Celia's building and parted ways with Meryem, with the promise—delivered between double hugs and kisses on both cheeks—that they would see each other again soon. Meryem said something to Umut that brought color to his cheeks and made him nod quickly as if trying to hurry the end of the moment along, but Eve didn't trouble herself with trying to guess what the content of Meryem's words might be. Not only did she not speak Turkish, but she knew better than to assume any conversation she couldn't understand was about her. A professional lifetime of literal code-switching had taught her that.

With one final goodbye to Meryem, Eve and Umut started up the stairs to Enes and Celia's apartment. "So..." she began, giving him her warmest smile. "She's wonderful. It's great that you have her."

He nodded as he sighed. "It is. I'm grateful, of course, to have her so close." Then, so softly she almost didn't hear it, he grumbled. "I could do without the unsolicited opinions on my love life, but, hey. You win some, you lose some."

Eve fought the temptation to ask him to elaborate, ultimately letting the fact that she was out of breath from their quick pace up the stairs lull her into silence. Before she fully knew what was happening, Umut was knocking on a familiar door and her old friend was opening it with a broad grin on her face.

"Hi guys!" cried Celia, smiling at Umut and pulling Eve in for a hug. "How did it go? How's the cat?" She pulled back, looking at them in puzzlement. "Does he have a name? I can't keep calling him 'the cat.'"

Umut stepped inside, where Enes was waiting to greet him. "We settled on Orca. Well, Eve did, actually, and I couldn't think of a better name."

"Orca!" Celia shook her head. "I love it. What do you think, Badem?" She looked down at the cat that was winding its way through her legs. "I think she approves," she said with a nod as she looked back up at Eve.

The five of them—because, after all, a noble creature like Badem had to be included in the headcount—made their way into the kitchen, where a feast awaited them. Eve felt her stomach rumble at the sights and smells there, the assortment of grilled meats and mouthwatering side dishes.

"Everything looks so good," she said, taking a deep breath. "Smells amazing, too. I have a feeling I am about to eat my body weight in delicious Turkish delicacies."

The four of them took their seats, digging in as they passed the dishes around the table in turn. Umut was next to Eve, his presence tugging some part of her awareness towards him even when she was deep in conversation with Celia.

By the time Umut was preparing to go home, Eve had felt the earth shift beneath her feet. It was as if the reality she had existed in before, even the reality she had existed in when she had arrived in Istanbul that same day, had been replaced by a new one. In that new reality, Celia was still her best friend, but they had morphed into a different kind of friendship that had expanded to include Enes and Umut. They were a couple of couples, a foursome who ate meals together and shared all of life's major moments...but which inevitably broke down into two separate pairings. It was clear enough that Celia and Enes were attached at the hip, and it seemed only natural that Eve should find herself magnetized to Umut's side as well.

It was more than a little disorienting, not only because she had never felt herself this swept up in an attraction to someone, but because that attraction felt different. It had legs. It had staying power if she would let it, and it felt like something other than what it so clearly was. She had a crush. What was so strange about that? Clearly she needed to retire to the guest room and sleep for at least eleven hours before she had herself believing she really had stumbled onto her other half or, even worse, saying something like that out loud.

"Oh, Umut," said Celia at the door. "Are you available to help with some wedding stuff tomorrow?" She winced apologetically, but when he nodded, Eve was almost sure she saw a devilish glint in her old friend's eye. "Great. I have more to do than I can take on myself, so I was thinking maybe I could give a few items on the list to you and Eve as well. Would you mind? I'd send her on her own, but—"

"I don't mind." Umut's words were directed at Celia, but his gaze was locked on Eve. "It would be my absolute pleasure."

As they said their goodnights, with Eve heading off to her room to sleep until life made sense again as soon as the door was closed behind Umut, she was only half aware of some unspoken communication happening between

Celia and Enes. Too tired to worry herself with what she might be missing, she closed the door behind her, leaving tomorrow to worry about itself.

Eleven

In the light of a new day, Celia's mastermind plan became clearer. The two friends were drinking their morning coffee while Celia asked Eve a lot of searching questions about the time she had spent with Umut, her eyes traveling over Eve's face while listening to her responses as if gathering even the tiniest micro-movements to fuel her case for compatibility of these two near-strangers.

"Sorry, I have to ask," said Eve. "It seems, from where I'm sitting at least, like you're dialing up the pressure to set me up with Umut." She turned the handle of her mug on the table. "Actually, it seems like that's what everyone is trying to do, at least if you count Orca and Meryem as everyone. Maybe Enes too, since I'm guessing the two of you would have hatched a plan like this together." She looked at her friend then. "Last night I thought maybe I was imagining it. That it was the jet lag talking. But today, in the light of a new day, it sure seems like you are very curious about what I thought about Umut and how every moment was spent at his house and what I'm thinking of doing together with him today and if I think he has pretty eyes and—"

"I did *not* ask if you think he has pretty eyes," said Celia with indignation. "Give me a little credit."

"No," Eve conceded. "But am I way off base here, or are you definitely trying to work a little romance magic?"

Celia looked down at the table and pursed her lips. "There's a non-zero possibility that I'm projecting my own experience on you and trying to recreate it." She shrugged. "Maybe it's because I'm about to get married and I'm remembering how it all began with me and Enes and Badem and...I don't know. I guess I want that same thing for you. Would it be so terrible if I did?"

Eve sighed. "No, it wouldn't. Not at all. It seems like you have a really beautiful life here, and I'd be lying if I said it didn't feel great last night to just imagine myself being a part of it." She looked at Celia then, willing her expression to convey the full depth of her seriousness. "But on the tiniest of chances that there could be something between me and Umut, it isn't going to blossom under this level of scrutiny. If anything, you're going to give us a complex and the end result will be nothing but awkward glances and stilted conversation. I'm pretty sure that isn't how things worked out for you and Enes, and it's definitely not how they're going to work out for me."

Celia had the decency to look sheepish. "That's...actually a really good point. I didn't think of it that way." She nodded once. "Okay, then. So...how do you want me to play it? What do you want me to do? Should I call him and cancel the errands today?"

Eve's stomach dropped. "Oh, no," she hurried to answer. "That's not necessary at all. That would just make things weird, wouldn't it? No, I'm happy to spend the day with him, but just…" She sighed. "Maybe give this thing room to breathe. I'm not saying there's no chance I'm going to let this little crush I have on him develop into something more, but—"

"So you do like him?" Celia's eyes had lit with eager expectation.

Eve huffed out a laugh. "Of course I do! That was never in question. Umut is great and kind and funny and handsome and…" She let herself trail off. "What's not to like, really? Just…let me spend the day with him and let's see how it goes. Okay?"

Celia nodded, her face the picture of emotional confusion. She was clearly trying to convey the seriousness of her respect for Eve's wishes while at the same time she had a shit-eating grin forcing its way across her visage. Eve would have snapped a picture of it if she'd had her phone within reach, but she settled instead for laughing at her friend.

"You're ridiculous," she said, "and I love you very much."

"I love you too," said Celia, reaching over to squeeze her hand. "And I hope you have the best day." She wiggled her eyebrows a couple of times and then clamped her lips together. "Sorry. That was the last teasing from me, I promise. For now, at least."

The last words came out so quietly Eve almost thought she had imagined them.

Twelve

U mut and Eve's task for the day was picking up table
linens on the other side of the city.

He had picked her up in the late morning, and after a
few hours of debate over the difference between eggshell
and cream napkins, they both agreed it was time to take
a break, preferably with food, beverage, and somewhere
comfortable to sit. And of course, Eve wouldn't say no to
a nice view of the city, either.

Umut took her to a quaint cafe with a nice view of
Galata Tower, and as they sat, waiting for their coffees and
sandwiches to arrive, he looked over the list Celia had given
them.

"There are still a few more things we need to pick up,"
he said, as his eyes traversed the paper one more time. "We
can finish it all today if we put our heads down, or we can
make another day of it and do it tomorrow. I mean, if you
aren't opposed to spending more time together." Was it
her imagination, or were the tips of his ears turning red
as he still pointedly studied the list without looking up at
her?

"Tomorrow is fine," she said, playing it as coolly as she could while at the same time feeling a disproportionate thrill at the thought of more time with Umut. "I mean, I guess I should check with Celia and make sure there isn't some other task she needs me for." She swallowed with a gulp. "But I'm sure she'll be okay with it."

That was how it began, and from there, Eve and Umut slipped naturally into spending their days together. Every wedding-related errand either of them was tasked with became a perfect task for two, and it was the shortest time before she found herself unable to imagine a day without him.

Celia had been entirely too amenable to the idea of missing out on quality time with her best friend. While Eve intermittently wrestled with guilt that she should be spending more time with Celia, she couldn't help but notice that every time Umut picked her up in the morning, Celia had that same grin on her face, and that she was putting less and less effort into hiding it with every passing day.

A week into Eve's visit, the two best friends planned a girls' night out, an evening for the two of them to visit a local wine bar, eat some light snacks, and talk about anything and everything that struck their fancy.

"Are you sure?" Eve had asked. "It's, like, a week until your wedding. If you want to bring Enes along, I definitely won't mind. Believe it or not, I'm actually a big fan of your future husband."

"Absolutely no boys aloud," Celia had responded with a resolute shake of her head. "I have a whole lifetime to spend with Enes, and you and I have things to talk about."

The two of them were getting ready side by side, sharing the bathroom mirror just like in the old days, and Celia bumped her hip into her friend. "I feel like I've barely seen you."

Eve frowned. "I'm sorry about that. I know it's nice to have help sorting out all the errands, but it's not great that I've been gone so much. I feel like a teenager, spending my summer vacation chasing boys around rather than actually enjoying quality time with my family."

"Nonsense! No way." This head shake was even firmer. "I'm glad you have someone to hang out with while I send you on wild goose chases all over town, and I'm even gladder that you're enjoying his company." She wrinkled her forehead apologetically. "I also feel like I owe you big time for all the errands I'm running. It, unfortunately, hasn't turned out to be a great time to have a wedding, considering that work is the opposite of what I expected it to be."

Celia was an efficiency expert, and she had been running her own consultancy for years. While she had planned to take time off for the wedding—and she still had a couple weeks off after the ceremony for a much-anticipated honeymoon—even more leads had been coming through than usual lately. It seemed like every evening when Eve came back to the apartment, Celia was more exhausted and had even more on her plate for the next day. Even though she loved what she did, it didn't change the fact that she was in need of a break.

Grateful that the topic had turned to work and away from Umut, Eve nodded. "I can't believe how in-demand you are." She applied another coat of mascara to her eyelashes, then tilted her head to the side in thought. "I mean, obviously, I can. I know you're good at what you do. Have known that since college and probably even before. Do you have any idea how you're going to change things when you get back from your honeymoon? I'm pretty sure if you keep working like this, you and Enes are never going to see each other, and we all know that isn't exactly the recipe for a stellar first year of marriage."

Celia looked deadly serious as she shook her head. "Trust me, it's on my radar. I know I don't want my marriage to start like that, and I also know I can't afford to have my business crumble right now. I just need to hold on a little longer, and if things don't start making more sense soon, then, well…" She trailed off, leaving both of them in mystery as to what the future held if her stress levels didn't change soon.

"I'm sorry to bring it up," said Eve, dabbing on a coat of lip gloss and then checking herself one last time in the mirror. "If there was anything I could do to help, I would. I hope you know that."

Something crossed Celia's face, but it was gone as quickly as it had come. "You already are," she said with a slightly forced smile. "Without your help, this wedding would be half planned at best."

As they made their way out the apartment and down the street to the restaurant—because when it came to two old friends drinking wine and catching up, being within walking distance was a must—Eve tried to shake off the heaviness of her concerns for her friend. They were supposed to enjoy their evening together, spend it reminiscing and laughing and essentially doing anything but feeling stressed about work and finances. But the thing about old friends was that even if you could put on a fake smile and convince most of the world that everything was okay, the ones that knew you best would always see through it.

And that was exactly what was happening with Eve and Celia.

On the street outside the bar, Eve stopped with her hand on Celia's arm. "I can't pretend I don't know you're stressed, Cee. And I don't think you would want me to either." She gave her oldest friend a small smile. "But I also trust you will talk to me about it whenever you want to. That you know you can do that. So just...don't forget that I'm here for you. That I'll always help you however I can. And...well, I know it's a weird thing to say when your friend is about to get married, but, anyway...men come and go, but friends are forever. Right?"

Celia gave her a watery smile. "Thank you, Eve. I don't know what I would do without you." She sighed. "And I will talk to you more about this soon. Just as soon as I have some time to actually think it through. In the meantime, I could actually use some girl talk. So if you want to tell me all about your crush on Umut, I promise to kick up my heels and giggle and stop looking like I'm carrying the weight of the world on my shoulders. Deal?"

Eve nodded. "Deal."

They made their way inside and found the perfect table—a spot where they could hear each other above the noise of the crowd and do some people-watching at the same time. After placing their drink order, Celia leaned back against the seat and gave her old friend a genuine smile. "So," she began with an encouraging nod, "tell me all about your week with Umut. All the details, please."

Despite herself, Eve could feel a swarm of butterflies in her low belly. "It's been…well, it's been really fun spending so much time with him. He's great, you know."

"Of course." Celia nodded. "The whole family is, at least everyone that I've met so far. But what do you *do* together? Does he know you like him? Like…that you *like* like him?" She winced. "I know I sound like a teenager, but you do *like* like him, right?"

Even as part of her was about to deny it, Eve found herself shaking her head in the affirmative. "I do. And it probably isn't even because you teased me about it at the beginning and therefore…I don't know…willed it into existence." She sighed. "Umut is just fun to be around. He listens and he cares far more than I typically expect a man to, though, that's probably not saying much since the bar is literally on the floor. And then there's the whole thing with Orca. The way he just took him home so easily, took on that responsibility. He's easy to talk to, and it goes without saying that he's easy to look at, and the two of us just don't run out of interesting stories or secrets to share or things that make us both laugh. I look forward to seeing him every day, and I can't imagine ever getting tired of him."

Celia's eyes had gone wider and wider as Eve had spoken. When Eve had finished her monologue, Celia nodded once. "I see," she said. "So you've got it bad then. *Crush* was probably the wrong word." She reached across the table and squeezed Eve's hand. "Thanks for telling me."

And just like that, the conversation moved on to other things. The two friends talked about Celia's family coming for the wedding, about the relatives who needed to be kept apart and the ones to might misrepresent the entire Long contingent to the Turkish side of the family and who should be monitored as a result. They shared about the projects that were keeping them busy at work—thanks to her long morning spent with Umut, Eve had spent a few late evenings catching up with her work projects.

Apart from the beginning, there was a noticeable lack of "girl talk," at least of the variety that would have them failing the Bechdel test. Celia didn't need to give Eve any updates on her relationship with Enes, considering that the three of them were all living under the same roof, and she had been happy to move on quickly from talking about Umut. Only the smallest part of Eve was tempted to be miffed that her "crush" had been dismissed so quickly, while the other, much larger, part of her was just happy to be spending time with her friend like nothing had changed and they were just two teenagers living out their dream.

"You know," she began, as the thought occurred to her. She gestured between them. "Look at the two of us. I mean, I know life isn't perfect and work can be stressful and blah blah blah..." She lifted her glass, tipping it towards Celia. "But aren't we kind of living the dream? I mean, the life we imagined back in middle school was full of glitz and glamor and very little substance. We watched the movies and read the magazines and decided we wanted to be 'thirty, flirty, and thriving.' I think we did even better than that, though. Look at you! You live in probably the coolest city in the world, you started your own business, and you're about to get married to your dream man."

Celia nodded along. "And don't forget about Badem. I also have the best cat, and I feel that would be very important to thirteen-year-old Celia."

Eve sucked in a breath. "Badem is great, but I might have to say she's tied for being the best cat. Orca is pretty darn amazing too. Did I tell you about the other day when he dropped his toy at my feet and waited for me to toss it like he wanted to play fetch?" She smiled at the memory. "He's so cute. Never thought I would say that about a cat, and yet here we are."

When she looked up, she found her old friend studying her with something that looked like suspicion. "What?" she asked. "I can think a cat is cute without it meaning something deep and profound and life-changing."

"Of course you can." Celia nodded. "Even if it does feel a bit like déjà vu, revisiting the beginning of my relationship with Enes."

"Just because you ended up finding a happily ever after that included a man, a cat, and Istanbul doesn't mean the same is going to happen for me." In an effort to convince Celia that she was sincere, she forced her smile to spread wider than felt natural. "And it's okay, really."

"If you say so." Celia's smile was more genuine. She nodded towards their empty glasses. "Another round?"

Thirteen

The night before Enes and Celia's wedding arrived with a speed that rivaled the approach of the first day back at work after a long weekend. The day had consisted of multiple trips to the airport to collect Celia's family members and plenty of last-minute errands. Eve had just finished getting Celia's aunt Trisha checked in to a hotel close to the wedding salon when she nearly collided with Umut as she exited the lobby.

"Whoa!" he called, his hands coming to rest on her upper arms to steady her. "You okay?" His eyes searched hers, and when she nodded, he gave her a warm smile. He tipped his head towards the hotel, which was now positively brimming with members of the Long family. "Was that the last of them? It seems like I've barely seen you today, what with all the running around."

The butterflies in her belly perked up with his comment. *So he had noticed her absence,* she thought, wondering, despite herself if he had felt it as keenly as she had.

She shook her head. "One final trip. Grandma Long is, for some inexplicable reason, traveling by herself and arriving the latest of them all."

He nodded, looking at the hotel again. "And she's staying there? Not with Celia and Enes?"

Eve chewed on her lower lip. "She's supposed to be staying at the hotel since I'm in Celia's guest room. But now that you mention it, that seems totally wrong. I shouldn't be hogging the bride the night before her wedding, especially not when her grandmother should be there." She felt panic threatening to overtake her. "Why didn't I think of this before? What should I do?" She turned back towards the hotel. "Maybe I can change the reservation to my name? But what if her grandma doesn't want that? What if she's one of those grandmas who definitely needs a hotel room of her very own and would hate to be relegated to the guest room?" She sighed. "And why didn't I think of this before? What is wrong with me?"

"Eve." At the sound of Umut's calm tone, she turned to face him, his hands once again anchoring her back to the earth. "It's okay. You didn't do anything wrong. If you want, you can leave the choice up to Celia's grandmother. You don't have to decide anything for her."

"No, but if I tell her she can stay in the guest room when it's already full of my clothes, she's going to be too polite to choose that even if she wants it."

"Right." He smiled at her. "That's why, if you want, you're going to move your things to my place. I have a guest room, too, and you're more than welcome to it. Then Celia's grandma will be free to choose whatever makes her most comfortable. You can even change the sheets and get the room all set for her."

"Oh." Eve blinked at him then, processing his words. "Oh. Right. Yes. I could do that." Her anxiety about her social misstep gone, that nervous energy needed a new place to go, and it found it easily. Though the problem of Grandma's comfort had been taken out of her hands, now she had a new problem.

Was she really going to be staying at Umut's apartment? The two of them? Alone? Unchaperoned?

She almost laughed at the voice in her head that seemed to think she was an unmarried lady in a Regency novel. She hadn't had a chaperone of any kind since her last field trip.

But even if it was a hilarious question, the concern underneath it was very real. An overnight visit, even if the two of them were staying in separate rooms, was something entirely different than any other time they had spent together so far.

"It's just…" she began, hesitating. "Well, I should check with Celia, shouldn't I? I don't want to offend her by just disappearing."

Umut nodded earnestly. "Of course. I don't want her to think I'm trying to steal her best friend, either. Why don't I head home and make up the spare bed just in case, and then you can let me know what the verdict is?"

"That sounds great. Oh, and thanks." She let out a small, nervous laugh. "I should have said that already. I do appreciate the offer, though. No matter what happens."

"Of course." He pulled her in for a quick peck on the cheek—one on each cheek, of course, which continued to catch Eve by surprise every time—and then gave her a small wave as he set off in the direction of his apartment.

Eve made the journey back to Enes and Celia's apartment in record time, just barely stopping herself from muttering out loud as she worked her way through what had just happened. Why hadn't they already thought about where Celia's grandmother should stay? Or had they, and she had been insistent on staying at the hotel? Was this something she was supposed to have already thought about? Did it fall under the umbrella of her maid of honor duties?

And underneath all of those concerns, of course, there lurked an entirely different set of bubbling worries. What did an overnight stay at Umut's apartment mean? Was this the prelude to a pre-wedding hookup? That wasn't something she had considered, and as much as she liked him, it didn't change the fact that Eve Shields didn't do casual hookups. And if Umut was being sneaky, was stacking the deck in favor of just that happening, then that might even make her whole crush on him evaporate in a puff of smoke...

"Don't assume his intention, Eve," she mumbled to herself. "It's good to be aware of the potential, but we mustn't assume Umut is a master of the art of seduction when it is entirely possible that he was just being kind. Courteous. Thoughtful. Helpful." She huffed out a laugh as she shook her head at herself. "All words which would describe every interaction we—and who is this royal we, anyway?—have had with him."

Inside the apartment, she found Celia steaming her wedding dress. She took the steamer from her friend and made short work of it, no sign of a wrinkle in the silky gown's long skirt.

Celia's eyes widened at Eve's accomplishment. "Well, then," she said. "I guess that's settled." She looked up at her old friend with a curious smile. "What's going on? You came running in here like you were on a mission."

"I am." Eve nodded. "It's your grandmother. I just realized that she's supposed to be staying in the hotel, but it feels so wrong to me to have her there when she should be staying here with you. I'm going to give up the room and let her choose. Umut is getting his guest room ready, so...yeah." Her final sentence rushed out, only to end abruptly without a complete thought.

Celia startled. "You're...giving Grandma the choice between my guest room or Umut's? I'm sorry, I think I missed something."

Eve could feel her cheeks burning as she shook her head. "No. Er...Umut is getting his guest room ready for me, so your grandma can choose between the hotel and your guest room. I was going to just go pack up my things and get the room ready, but then I figured I should tell you first."

"Right. Gotcha." Celia was looking down at the table, her eyes moving across its surface as if she were reading something written there. She looked like she was about to say something, but then stopped herself with a nod. "I think it's a great idea, and I really appreciate you and Umut thinking of it." She gave Eve a broad smile then. "I wouldn't have asked you to leave, couldn't have even imagined it. But I do think Grandma will really appreciate having the choice." She got to her feet then. "Would you like me to help you get your things together?"

Eve barely managed to suppress her shock at how quick Celia was to accept her offer. Wasn't her friend supposed to insist the move was unnecessary? That her grandmother would be fine sticking with the original plan? But she reminded herself that she had made the offer in good faith and it wouldn't make any sense at all to take it back now. "That would be perfect," she said with a smile. "Thank you so much."

Fourteen

In the early evening, Eve was waiting outside Umut's apartment, suitcase in hand. Celia was doing the final airport run to pick up her grandmother, with Enes accompanying her, and Eve was suddenly feeling...adrift. She had been a part of her friend's world for nearly two weeks, had made herself at home in that same friend's home, and even though she had spent plenty of time with Umut, there was something about waiting outside his door with everything she had brought to Istanbul that felt wrong.

It wasn't that it felt wrong to be spending time with Umut, or even that being away from her best friend on the night before her wedding wasn't exactly how they had imagined this particular milestone unfolding all those years ago. It was more the fact that it felt so oddly familiar to be spending the evening at Umut's house, far too comfortable and natural to be right. Not that she felt comfortable about navigating the tension that was between them, the "will-they-won't-they" energy that had been making her feel like a character in a sitcom for most of her stay in the city.

She lifted her hand to knock, but before she could make contact with the door, it opened and Umut was there, his eyes widening at the sight of her. "You're here!" He seemed flustered. "I was just coming out to meet you. Walk you over." He eyed her suitcase. "Help you with that thing, but I can see you didn't need it."

She smiled as she handed the suitcase over to him. "You're welcome to it now. If I don't have to schlep that thing anywhere again until I head to the airport, that will be considered a win in my book."

Umut frowned slightly as he brought the suitcase inside, with her close behind. "When are you leaving? I now realize I never asked you that important question."

"Oh. Well, I mean, I'm leaving on Monday," she said, hurrying to explain herself. "I didn't mean I was going to stay with you until then."

He held up a hand to stop her. "No, I wasn't asking in that way. You would, of course, be more than welcome to stay as long as you liked." He smiled then. "I was really just asking how much longer we get to keep you, but I haven't exactly been in a big hurry to think about you leaving. Maybe it felt like if I just didn't mention it, then we could pretend it wasn't happening."

"Ah." She felt her pulse picking up as she nodded at him. "Yeah, I know what you mean. It is, unfortunately, happening, though. No miraculous turns of event or forces of nature have conspired to keep me here indefinitely, so back to St. Louis I go."

"Well, it's definitely our loss." He had taken her suitcase into an empty bedroom, leaving it just inside the door. "And we hope you'll be back again soon." He shook his head once. "No, I should say *I* hope you'll be back soon. As much as I like to think I represent the entire city, I should just speak for myself."

She gave him a small smile. "I hope so, too. I don't actually want to go, but I think that's normal when you travel far away from home. It's easy to imagine a new life, a new reality...but then your old job, your bills, your commitments back home come calling. Most people don't get to turn their vacations into one-way plane tickets, after all."

"No, I guess they don't." He gestured towards the bed. "This is where you'll be staying. I changed the sheets, left you a towel just there. If there's anything else you need, just ask." He seemed to be in a hurry to leave, his feet already taking him towards the door. "I'll give you some time to get settled in, then I thought we could...I don't know, have dinner or a movie or whatever you want? Are there any pre-wedding maid of honor and photographer traditions I should be aware of?"

"I don't think it's particularly traditional for the maid of honor and photographer to spend the night before the wedding together." She worried her lower lip for a second before catching herself, forcing a smile. "Of course, it's also tradition for the bride and groom not to see each other the night before, so I think we're pretty much throwing the rule book out the window." There was a part of her that wanted to mourn the old idea that the two best friends should be having a sleepover the night before one of their weddings, whispering late into the night about how everything was going to change. But then she remembered that they'd been having sleepovers every night for the past two weeks and that it surely wouldn't be the last time one of them crashed in the other's guest room.

So instead she just smiled at Umut. "Give me two minutes to settle in, and then I'm all yours." She felt her cheeks heat instantly at her words. "I mean, we'll decide together what to do then. But food, a movie…it all sounds good. I have no last minute wedding-related duties to attend to. Do you?"

"No, I'm good too." He gestured towards the living room with his thumb. "I should go see what Orca's up to, anyway. He's been entirely too quiet since you arrived, and that's likely to mean trouble."

As Umut made his way out of the room and Eve began to arrange her things, hanging up her dress for the next day so that it wouldn't wrinkle, she heard a rustling sound from underneath the bed. Dropping to her knees, she looked into the darkness to see two glowing eyes staring back at her. "Well, there you are," she cooed to Orca, tapping on the ground with her fingers to entice him out. "Your dad's looking for you."

The cat emerged, a few dust bunnies stuck to his back that Eve quickly brushed away. "You're trying to make him look bad? Reveal that he didn't actually push aside the bed and vacuum every square inch of the room?" She tsked at the cat. "As if that would be enough to scare me off," she murmured.

A throat cleared from the doorway and she turned to see Umut there, looking slightly apologetic. He nodded towards the cat. "I heard you talking in your cat-slash-baby voice, and I figured you had found him. I can take him off your hands if you'd like."

She shook her head. "It's okay, we're just about finished here." She narrowed her eyes at him then. "And how do you know that's the voice I use with babies? I'll admit to speaking to Badem and Orca that way, but I'm confident you've never seen me interact with a human baby."

"Just a guess," he said with a smile. "Though clearly I shouldn't have assumed."

Eve replaced her suitcase on the floor as she got to her feet. "Right. Agreed. Well, that's enough of that. I'm just now realizing that I am super hungry, so…"

"Say no more," said Umut with one firm nod. "Your wish is my command."

Fifteen

Two hours later, Eve could barely keep her eyes open. She and Umut had feasted on a takeout order of fried chicken—nothing better than greasy food the night before she wanted to look her best—while watching *Jaws*—"it's high time Orca met another apex predator," Umut had said. She had chosen the food with the requirement that he choose the movie, and they had both been pleased to find the other's wishes aligned quite nicely with their own. Now, the credits were playing on the screen and there were only crumbs left on the coffee table.

Eve stretched before quickly covering her mouth to stifle a yawn. Orca was asleep on the couch between them, his head resting on Eve's thigh while his back paws were making contact with Umut's leg. She didn't want to move, didn't want the evening to end...and yet she knew it was a dream that was destined to slip away. It wasn't as if sitting there on the couch for a few more minutes would change the future, rewrite it with a reality where she and Umut could be together, where this kind of evening could be the norm for them.

And so she got to her feet, slipping Orca's chin off her leg and back onto the couch, and smiled down at the man and his cat. "Good night, Umut," she said. "It was a lovely evening. Thank you for letting me stay."

He looked like he wanted to say more, but simply nodded and wished her sweet dreams. When she slipped inside her bedroom door a moment later, he was still right where she had left him on the couch.

As she closed the door behind her, there was a pang of longing. Only the responsible part of herself, the part that wanted to be well rested before her best friend's wedding and also did not want to get her heart broken if she could avoid it, was satisfied as the door clicked shut and she leaned back against it. There was another part of her—a much larger part now, that seemed like it had been growing in size for days—that wanted to march right back to the couch, to announce that she had never watched any of the *Jaws* sequels and suggest a marathon to last the rest of the night.

That part of her also wanted to trade spots with Orca, to stretch out across the couch and cross the invisible boundary between her and Umut. She wanted to sit so close the sides of their thighs were touching or to stick her toes under his leg or stretch her legs across his lap...something that felt so foreign and forbidden and yet so right and comfortable.

But she didn't do any of that. She pushed herself off the door and alone into the night. Her only mission was to get some rest, to resist giving into temptations, and to arrive at Celia's wedding day with her heart intact.

The only problem, she thought, as she pulled the blanket up to her chin, *is that even without taking any action, my heart is already involved. Already in danger of being broken when that moment comes where I know I'll never see Umut again.* And there wasn't a thing she could do about it.

Sixteen

The morning of the wedding dawned with an emergency—*didn't they all?* thought Eve as she answered her phone far too early.

"Hello?" she grumbled into the device. "Is something wrong?"

Celia's words tumbled out too quickly for Eve to understand. She forced herself up to a sitting position as she rubbed her eyes. "Say that again?"

"It's all wrong," said Celia. "We can't just leave her at home, right? I mean, she's the reason we met in the first place, and it just doesn't make sense to get married without her there—"

Eve cleared her throat as realization dawned. "Hang on a second," she said. "Are you talking about Badem?"

"Of course I am!" Celia sounded like she was near tears. "It's just wrong not to have her there today. I mean, if anything, she should be the officiant. Or the flower girl. Or at least in some kind of place of honor! Leaving her at home? That just seems like a slap in the face."

Eve smiled to herself. "Well, my dear, I won't tell you that you've lost your mind because I understand that your wedding day is generally a pretty emotionally volatile day." She heard faint protestations on the other end of the line, something to the effect that "not telling" someone something while still saying the thing that you "aren't saying" is the same as saying it, but an idea was already blossoming in her mind. "Let me get Umut up and bring him over there. You guys just start getting ready, okay? We'll take care of it all."

Twenty minutes later, Eve and Umut had slipped Orca into his new travel carrier and were out the door, on their way to Enes and Celia's apartment. Umut had been quick to get on board with Eve's plan, and it had even been his idea to bring the young cat along to keep Badem company.

"I hope they made extra coffee," he said, stifling a yawn. "I have a feeling it's going to be a long day."

She felt a pang of guilt for rushing him out of the apartment so quickly, but then reminded herself that she was not, in fact, doing this for selfish motivations. Unless easing Celia's wedding day jitters could be considered a selfish motivation, but in that case, she would gladly wear that particular crown.

Instead, she just smiled up at Umut, blinking at him with what she knew he would read as mischief in her eyes. "It's nice to see you first thing in the morning," she said. "Before you've had a chance to put on your face, I mean." She reached for his face before she could stop herself, her fingers trailing lightly up his cheeks. "So sleepy," she said softly.

Oh, she could play it all off as a joke, but that didn't mean she wasn't thrilled to be spending the first moments of her day with Umut. In fact, she *had* to play it all off as a joke, or else she was in danger of calling the airline to cancel her flight, sinking right back onto his couch, putting her feet up on the coffee table, and staying there until archaeologists in the distant future had to puzzle over her remains.

Rather than open that particular can of worms, Eve picked up her pace and felt Umut quicken his beside her. With little room for conversation—and the quiet of the still sleeping neighborhood around them—they were ringing the bell to be let into Enes and Celia's apartment before more than a few moments had passed.

Before Eve had the chance to catch her breath, the buzzer sounded, the door unlocked, and Umut had pushed it open, holding it for her to pass. The two of them, along with a stoic, silent Orca, climbed the stairs and arrived at an open apartment door where a frazzled Celia and only slightly calmer Enes were waiting for them. Enes was holding a wiggling Badem in his arms, and Celia was petting the cat's head lightly with one hand while her other fingers played along the doorjamb.

"Hi guys." Eve smiled as she took in the scene, her friend's anxiety so palpable it was in danger of spilling over into her reality as well. "How's...uh...how's it going over here?"

"Come inside," said Celia, stepping out of the doorway. "It's...well, it's just wedding stress, I'm pretty sure. But that doesn't mean I don't feel like my soul has poison ivy."

"It's not about me!" Enes called from further down the hallway, where he and Umut were making their way to the kitchen while the women lingered in the doorway. "I already checked and double checked, and I can assure you that I am not the cause of these particular worries."

"That's true," said Celia, a genuine smile crossing her face for the first time. "I'm so excited to be marrying Enes today. But suddenly there are so many details that have to fall into place in order for me to marry him, and I feel like I'm messing them all up. I mean...are we doing all the traditions that are meaningful to his family, while also incorporating enough of my family and culture that no one is going to be offended? And how could I plan this whole day without thinking about Badem? She's such a big part of our story, and we don't even have, like, a photograph of her to put in the place of honor." She gave Eve a sad smile then. "I know it isn't realistic to bring her to the wedding salon. But not having her represented there at all just feels like a slap in the face."

Enes poked his head back in from the kitchen. "If you can help reassure my very-soon-to-be-wife, Eve, that there is no need for this day to be perfect and that as long as it ends with the two of us married to each other it will be a smashing success, that would be much appreciated." He started to pull away, but then reappeared. "Oh, and that Badem is very excited for her playdate with Orca. To the point where she probably won't even notice we're missing. On second thought, don't emphasize that particular fact too much or it might set off an entirely new set of emotions."

Celia let out a watery laugh. "I'm a mess, aren't I?"

"Not even a little." Enes shook his head, and the moment that passed between the two of them was so baldly honest, so stripped of any pretense or game-playing, that Eve had to look away. "Everything about you adds up to the woman I love, and I wouldn't change a hair on your head. Or a thought in your head, for that matter, since those seem to be the origin of today's worries."

"It's true." Celia looked away from her fiance and sighed as she slipped her hands into Eve's. "I think when this is over, I'm going to sleep for a month. And I'm sure by tomorrow morning everything that's stressing me out is going to feel like a distant memory." She shrugged. "But that doesn't do me a bit of good right now. Still going to stress about getting it right."

"And I would frankly be worried about you if you didn't," said Eve with a warm smile as she guided her friend towards the kitchen. "I'd wonder who this chill, calm woman is and what she had done with my best friend." She tipped her head to the side, unable to stop her next words from spilling out of her mouth. "I mean, I feel like your career would be in danger of falling apart if you chilled out too much, you know? It's like that stress is an asset to your success."

All the activity in the room stopped on a dime, as if a record had been scratched. Celia looked at her with wide, concerned eyes, and over her friend's shoulder Eve could see both men giving her head shakes and hand signals that told her to play it off, change the topic, or go back in time and unsay what she had just said.

She forced a weak laugh. "I don't mean it that way, Celia. It was a bad joke. I'm not telling you to stay stressed or else you'll have an even bigger stressor to deal with. I just meant that you're so good at paying attention to the details, that's all."

"Right." Celia's gaze darted to Enes, and he gave her a small shake of his head. "Anyway, should we go...start getting ready?"

Eve smiled. "You mean you don't have a minute by minute itinerary for the day?"

"Believe it or not, no. I need to be ready and at the wedding salon at three, but I can kind of take my time, I guess." She looked at Enes again. "Unless there's something I don't know about?"

He shook his head. "Nothing that I'm keeping from you. I can't promise the entire family is thinking the same way, but since I haven't heard any drumming yet, I think we're in the clear."

"Drumming?" Eve raised an eyebrow, gaze darting between everyone in the room.

"Don't worry about it," said Umut with a wink. "Come look at these two." He waved with his hand, and Eve saw for the first time that the door of Orca's cage was open and Badem had squeezed herself inside with him.

"Wow." Celia dropped to her knees in front of the cage, her hands clutching in front of her heart. "They are just the sweetest." When she looked up again, her eyes were brimming with tears.

"Oh. No. No, we can't have that." Enes shot to his feet, racing over to Celia to pull her to hers. "I know they're happy tears, or oh-it's-so-cute-I-can't-stand-it tears, but still. No." He brushed her hair behind her ear, a sudden smile sparking on his face. "Should I call Adnan? Invite Poppy to come spend the wedding here with these two?"

Celia gave him a watery nod, clearly unable to get another word out without losing herself with the rapidly cresting swell of emotions.

"Coffee!" cried Umut, making his way towards the counter. "And it is my expert opinion—I think we can all agree that I have been involved with the highest number of weddings—that eating a good breakfast the morning of the wedding is essential. We don't want a jittery bride or a groom who passes out because he forgot to eat."

As the four of them set to preparing breakfast, scrambling eggs and slicing cucumbers as if it were a carefully choreographed dance, Eve took in the relative silence from the rest of the apartment.

"Your grandma didn't stay here?" she asked Celia in a low voice. She didn't need to alert Umut to the fact that, apparently, their sleepover had been unnecessary.

Something flickered across Celia's face, and then, with a heavy sigh, she shook her head. "No, she didn't want to. She said she had really been looking forward to the tiny shampoos at the hotel and had a whole strategy for getting a few extra to take back home with her." She bit her lip. "Are you mad? You could have come here after she went to the hotel, but, to be honest, I kind of wanted to channel my inner Badem and do a little matchmaking. A little bit of forced proximity for you and Umut."

Without thinking, Eve blurted her response. "Not at all. If anything, I'm impressed. And if that isn't carrying the spirit of Badem with you on your wedding day while she stays at home and rolls around on catnip toys, then I don't know what is."

Seventeen

After they had all eaten their fill, Eve and Celia set about preparing for the big day. Despite Enes's family's insistence that they would be happy to pay for Celia and all the women close to her to have their hair and makeup done at a nearby beauty salon, Celia had been sure she preferred a quiet morning at home, with only her closest friend. Now that the day was here, Eve could tell she had made the right call. Badem was sitting on Celia's lap while Eve curled her hair, and the soothing purrs must be working wonders for Celia's nervous system because she finally seemed to have stopped jiggling her leg anxiously.

Enes and Umut had left after washing the dishes, one to prepare all of his photography equipment for the big day and the other to handle any and everything else. Enes had ducked back in briefly with a friendly neighbor in tow, a woman named Meredith who brought a small, friendly calico cat who seemed well acquainted with Badem already. The cat—Poppy, the woman had called her—was sleeping on the living room couch now with Orca, after the two of them had tired each other out with a fierce game of pouncing and chasing each other around the apartment.

Eve had been about to suggest that maybe turning the apartment into a kitty daycare hadn't been the right idea when all three cats, much like overtired toddlers, had abruptly abandoned their game and fallen asleep sharing two cushions on the couch, as if they hadn't just been taking turns hunting each other. Orca and Poppy were still passed out cold, while Badem had taken on her therapy cat role in the bedroom, comforting and grounding Celia while the preparations were underway.

"This is exactly why I couldn't go to a beauty salon," Celia was saying, looking down to scratch Badem's chin. "I mean, this is Turkey, so it's entirely possible the salon would come with a cat of its own." She sighed. "But it wouldn't be my cat, and so the effect wouldn't be the same."

The moment the friends were sharing was interrupted by a knock on the door. "Are you expecting anyone?" Eve asked, wondering if she had enough bobby pins for the cousin or college friend who might be about to enter.

"No one," said Celia with a shake of her head. "My family members are all set up with a custom tour of the closest sites—Meredith's boyfriend, Adnan, is showing them around. And I don't think any of Enes's family would be coming here now."

"Well, there's nothing to do but answer the door, I guess." Eve looked at her friend, hair half curled and with the still sleeping cat on her lap. "I'll get it."

Before Celia could stop her, Eve was out in the hallway and pulling open the door to find...

"Jasmine!" The cafe owner turned wedding caterer was standing in front of her, a wrapped package in her hands and a broad smile on her face. "What's up?" Eve asked, before dropping her voice so that Celia couldn't hear. "Is everything okay? There isn't a problem at the wedding salon, is there?"

"Not at all. Everything is great. I just, well...I have something special to deliver." She held up the package and nodded towards it. "Is Celia here?"

"She's right here!" Celia's voice called from the bedroom. "I'd come to you, but Badem says no. Plus, I'm holding a hot curling iron and have no where to put it."

Celia's eyes widened at the sight of the rectangular package in Jasmine's hands. "What's this? Is it a wedding photo album?" She shook her head. "No, that doesn't make sense. We haven't taken any of the photos yet because the wedding is today." She smiled, confusion evident in her features. "What is it?"

Jasmine took the curling iron out of Celia's hands, replacing it with the package. "Open it and find out. And before you get too excited and want to squeeze the life out of me...it's from Enes. I mean, I did make it. But it was his idea. So he's the one you should thank."

Celia frowned slightly. "Okay..." As she slipped the paper off the package, her jaw dropped and a gasp escaped her lips. "This is amazing."

She turned the object—Eve could see now that it was a canvas of some sort—to show the others, and Eve saw what had left her friend so speechless. It was an oil painting of Badem, painted in the style of a classic portrait of a member of a royal family, but the regal-looking cat was surrounded by beautiful bright flowers, colorful cat toys, and...

"Are those olives?" asked Eve, pointing to the green oblong spheres.

Jasmine nodded. "Of course. It wouldn't be a portrait of Badem if I didn't include some of her favorite things."

"Enes asked you to make this?" said Celia, as if just remembering what the woman had said.

"He did. He wanted to give it to you as a wedding present, in honor of the little matchmaker herself, but he sent a message last night asking if I would bring it this morning. He thought you might want to take it to the wedding salon with you, set it up somewhere there so that it would be as if Badem were actually there too and not at home playing with her friends."

"Oh, well...I mean..." Celia's words weren't quite coming out right, the emotion spilling out where her sentences couldn't. "It's perfect. Thank you."

"You're very talented," agreed Eve, nodding at Jasmine. "I can't imagine something like that being created by my two hands."

Jasmine's smile was humble. "I can't take all the credit. Your guy, Umut, had taken some really excellent photos of Badem, and that's what I used for the painting. If I had been trying to create this without that reference, it would be missing the energy and motion he had captured in those photos. He's really talented, too, you know."

"Oh, I definitely do." Eve was sure she was blushing now, the first heat she had felt at Jasmine referring to Umut as belonging to her roaring into full bloom with the intensity of the woman's persistent gaze. For someone she had only met two weeks prior, she sure did have a knack for reading the unspoken connections between two near-strangers-to-her that weren't intended for public consumption.

"Anyway, I'm going to head home and finish getting ready for the day," said Jasmine, beginning to move towards the hallway. "You two don't need anything, do you?" After they both insisted they were more than equipped for the task at hand, Jasmine gave one final nod, told them she'd see them at the wedding salon, and left.

"How are you feeling?" asked Eve. A vague and uncomfortable feeling washed over her as she realized it was the first time she had really asked her friend that question in the lead-up to the wedding. She had been spending so much time with Umut, so much energy swept up in her own feelings, that she had taken for granted that her best friend was only feeling the good kind of nerves about her wedding, that her feet were the furthest thing from getting cold at the thought of marrying Enes.

She needn't have worried though, judging by the beatific smile that had cemented itself across Celia's face. Something had changed in her demeanor since she had received Jasmine's artwork. "I'm good," she said. "So good." She held up the painting. "He knows me. Anticipates my feelings before even I do. Has been nothing but good and kind and loving ever since we began this relationship." She sighed deeply. "Any nerves I was feeling...well, it's just clearer than ever before that they don't matter at all. I'm marrying Enes today, and I am so excited about it."

"That's beautiful." Eve smiled back at her friend, sliding back into position behind her to finish curling her hair.

What would it feel like to have someone in her life that she could speak like that about? Would she know that for herself some day? Find someone who felt that much like home? And would the part of her that felt like Umut could be that person ever let her give up wondering what might have been with him and give her heart to someone else?

"What about you?" Celia had put her hand on Eve's, stopping her from engaging the curling iron as she turned to look up at her friend. "How are you feeling? I know it's *my day*"—she rolled her eyes at the expression—"but don't think that means I don't see what's going on with you. Are you okay? How's your heart?"

Eve forced a smile, shaking her head to convey a confusion she didn't feel. "I'm fine. What could possibly be on my mind when I'm here with you, about to watch my favorite friend marry her actual perfect match?"

Celia's gaze was unrelenting. "It's not unheard of for people's thoughts about their own relationship status to rise to the forefront during a wedding. And I know you well enough to know that spending the night at Umut's house and showing up here like you're some kind of bride and groom support team must have done a number on you. You were anticipating each other's moves and slotting so seamlessly into place beside each other that even a woman who's almost entirely consumed by her own impending wedding can't help but notice that there is something there. And I know I thought there was something there before, but after whatever happened last night—and you definitely owe me a story time about that, by the way—that *Something* probably deserves a capital S now."

"We'll talk about it, I promise." Eve nodded at her friend. "Nothing happened last night. Not whatever you're wiggling your eyebrows at me about, anyway. I can't deny that I like him. That *like* feels like the lamest word to describe whatever it is that I have the potential to feel for him." She shook her head, just once. "But nothing has changed that could unlock that. I'm here for your wedding, and after today, we start moving towards my departure at an alarmingly fast rate. I'm leaving, Cee. And I'm not young or naïve enough to think that a long-distance relationship would be a good idea."

"I understand," said Celia. "I won't push it."

And Eve thanked her, equal parts grateful to be moving on from the subject and wishing desperately that her friend wouldn't give up. That she would push the idea of Eve and Umut until its inevitability forced a new reality into existence.

Eighteen

Celia and Enes's wedding was beautiful, from the ceremony that blended both of their cultures to the hours spent dancing around the dance floor. Eve had been surprised to learn that most wedding ceremonies were short and sweet, that Celia and Enes's decision to have a few significant passages and poems read by loved ones and to share their vows with their family and friends was an uncommon one. Every word spoken, it seemed, magnified the magic in the air, the assurance they all shared that these two humans who had found each other against all odds were meant to be together.

The short and sweet ceremony ended with a kiss, one that was placed on Celia's forehead by her new husband while the Turkish side of the newly joined family cheered and the American side exchanged concerned glances with each other. Noting their hesitation, Celia chuckled. "It's supposed to be like that!" she reassured her loved ones. "It's part of the tradition, and PDA isn't super common."

"Oh, good!" her grandmother called back. "I thought it meant he just liked you as a friend, and this would be a rather inconvenient time to learn that."

Eve laughed and began to make her way over to Grandma Lila, Celia's grandmother. Though she had known the older woman for decades, she hadn't had the chance to speak with her yet on this side of the Atlantic.

"Hi, Grandma Lila," she said with a smile as she placed a light hand on her arm. "How are you? How was your trip? How's the hotel?"

"Eve! There you are! What's with all the questions, kiddo? Can't you at least give me a hug first?" After she pulled Eve towards her and wrapped her arms around her waist, squeezing tighter than she had any right to, Grandma Lila stepped back. "I'm fine, and so was my flight, and so is the hotel. I'm dying to know about you, though. When Celia told me you gave up the room at the house for me so you could sleep over at that handsome photographer's house, I realized I had never been prouder of her."

"What do you mean?"

"Well, doll, of course I wasn't going to stay in my Celia's apartment, and I can promise you she was well aware of that." Grandma Lila shook her head. "No, that would never have done. Celia knows—don't ask me how she does, that story is embarrassing for both of us, but it can't be helped now—I sleep in the nude and I get up to use the restroom more times each night than hungry dog checking to see if any new food has appeared in its bowl. That leaves a hotel as my only option, you see."

Eve forced herself not to smile as she memorized every quirk of the older woman's eyebrows as she spoke. Grandma Lila was nothing if not the quintessential storyteller, her knack for charming and shocking her audience equally impressive. "Well, that's good to know then," was all she managed to reply.

Celia's grandmother narrowed her eyes at her. "Oh, don't tell me you think my granddaughter was up to something diabolical, manipulating you like that. Everyone knows couples these days need a little push sometimes. If anything, I'm prouder of her for this little move than my own grandmother ever was of me." She tilted her head slightly, as if admitting to something in only the most begrudging of ways. "Of course, I didn't give a fig what that woman thought of me, and I would have been alarmed if I'd ever learned that she was pleased with the choices I made."

"We can't all be the picture of grandmotherly wisdom," said Eve, squeezing the older woman's hand. "Not like you."

Grandma Lila made a face. "I'll drink to that, but only if you promise never to say the phrase 'grandmotherly wisdom' again." She shivered with disgust. "If you want to copy all my one-liners down into a book and start a religion based on it, I'm okay with that. But if you want me to be a sweet little grandma sitting on her rocker, knitting sweaters for kittens, and saying the kind of shit that gets cross-stitched onto stupid little pillows, you're going to have to find another woman."

"Alright then, it's a deal," said Eve as she began to move away from Grandma Lila. She had just spotted Umut across the room, his camera gone from his neck for the first time that evening—and his eyes were on her.

He watched her as she moved across the room towards him, as if it were his gaze that was compelling her to cut such a direct line towards her goal. Whether it was something Grandma Lila had said or the wedding romance in the air, she only knew in that moment that she wanted to be near him and, for the first time in their acquaintance, she really didn't care what anyone who might be watching her, might be perceiving the feelings she was normally so careful to hide, would think. It was an occasion to celebrate love, and after Enes and Celia's beautifully vulnerable vows, there couldn't be a cynic left in the room.

Not even Eve could be cynical about love and weddings after serving as witness to her best friend's new beginning.

And that was how she found herself standing in front of Umut, smiling up at him as he smiled down at her, words tumbling out of her mouth before she could think twice.

"I like you," she said, with no trace of irony. "I'm glad I met you. And if I weren't about to leave, I would definitely suggest that we think about going on a proper date."

He nodded, though the faintest trace of something like resolution had flickered across his expression at her reminder that she would be leaving Turkey soon. "I would like that," he said, "because it's all the same for me, too. In fact, I would ask you to consider extending your stay—not making a joke about it, but really asking it—if I thought there was any chance it might work."

"Maybe in another life," she said with a sad smile.

"Maybe." He nodded. "But for tonight, at least, will you save a dance for me?"

Eve nodded to the dance floor, where the wedding guests were moving in circles, snapping their fingers along to the beat as they took small steps. "You mean this? I'm not generally a big dancer at weddings, but this I can handle."

He smiled then. "We can certainly do a bit of this, but I was also talking about dancing to one of the slow, romantic songs. You know, the kind where you stand really close to each other and sway from side to side and try to have a conversation, but it's too loud for that, so you kind of just end up hugging and rocking back and forth

"You described that so perfectly it's like you're inside my head." She grinned at him. "I will save a dance for you, for sure. As many as you want, in fact." She reached a hand towards his chest, to the place where his camera should be. "You aren't on photo duty any more?"

He shook his head. "I may be the photographer, but I'm the groom's cousin, too. I captured all the portraits, but I've got additional shooters for the candids. I'll keep an eye on things, but for all intents and purposes, I'm off work for the rest of the evening."

"That's good then." She swallowed, tipping her head towards the dance floor. "Shall we?"

Nineteen

They danced for hours. It was the simplicity of it, the structure of a Turkish wedding dance, that made it easy for Eve to lose herself in it. It wasn't like the club dancing or the American wedding dancing that she was so quick to avoid, the freestyle nature of it that started off as fun but quickly soured when she had used up all her go-to moves and had nothing interesting to contribute.

Instead, at this wedding, the style of dancing was largely restricted to taking small steps around a circle or oval full of her fellow wedding guests, while they all moved their arms and snapped their fingers, the smallness of the movements and the predictability of it all providing her with a feeling of security and structure that was completely foreign to her on a dance floor of any kind.

Umut stayed by her side as they danced with Enes and Celia, who were making their rounds to dance with all their guests. They danced with Grandma Lila, who darted enough mischievous glances between the two of them to generate speculation from even the most oblivious guests, and possibly even to generate enough electricity to power a neighborhood of the city.

Eve saw Celia's parents, snapping right along with Enes's mother, Jasmine and a man in a crisp button-down shirt who never left her side, and even Meredith, the woman she had met just that morning when she brought Poppy over to keep Orca and Badem company. Meredith, by the looks of it, hadn't even noticed the other people in the room, so dialed in was she to the man she had arrived hand-in-hand with who kept her laughing at least twice a minute.

To stop herself from making a comment about all the American women with their Turkish partners, she leaned closer to Umut and shouted, "What do you think the cats are doing now?"

"What?" he yelled back, shaking his head to show he hadn't caught a word of what she had said.

She leaned closer than before, her lips dangerously close to his ear, but before she could repeat her question, the music changed to a slow, romantic song, and the DJ was making an announcement.

Umut groaned, pulling a face. During the respite from the bumping pop tune that had just ended and before the new song could get well and truly underway, there was a moment where the two of them could hear each other speak. "He's calling all the couples to the floor." He held out a hand to her. "If you don't want to dance, don't want people talking about what the two of us dancing together during this particular song means...I can lead you back to your table."

But she just shook her head as she placed her hand in his. "I don't actually care what anyone thinks about it. It sounds like a nice song, and I'm not going to pass up the chance to dance to it with you. Who knows if we'll get another chance?"

They got into position, starting in that awkward frame that reminded her of middle school, her eyes trying to land somewhere less awkward than right on his—prolonged eye contact would only work with conversation, and they had already proved that was impossible at this volume level. Eve sighed then, and took one step closer to him, letting her cheek rest on his chest as his arms came around her, holding her close. She didn't care if that wasn't how everyone else was dancing, if all the other couples seemed to be performing a cookie cutter version of the same dance—one arm slightly extended, one on the other's shoulder and lower back, respectively. She listened instead to her body, to her heart, to what felt the most comfortable to her. And it was there, with her head pressed against Umut's heart, a place where she was sure she would have been able to hear it beating, if she could hear anything but the singer's voice, the piano, the recording that seemed to contain a full orchestra of instruments both familiar and foreign.

It was nice to be held, entirely unfamiliar to close her eyes against the observations of others and simply enjoy the closeness of another human being. And not just any human being, of course, but Umut. As happy as it had made Eve to witness her best friend's wedding, this moment right here was quickly becoming her favorite one from her trip to Turkey. This was the moment she would be revisiting on a long, cold night in St. Louis in the not-too-distant future.

When the song ended, she smiled back up at him before any of her protective defenses could slip back into place, before her eyes could dart away from his to see if anyone was watching her, was whispering about her, was judging her the way she had been so quick to judge true emotional vulnerability before. It was funny to think how critical she had been of love stories, how quick she had been to change the topic from a sweet proposal story to the cost of the average wedding, pulling faces that made it clear to anyone—brides' feelings be damned—just how much of a waste she felt it was.

In this moment, though, she got it. It wasn't as if she would say yes to Umut if he proposed right now; she was rational enough to recognize that some impulses could have lasting consequences. But she could see, could feel, that the spark between them would need very little encouragement to turn into a roaring flame. And she dared to wish that such a thing were possible, that her "real" life didn't require her to return to St. Louis, that there was some easy way she could stay put in Istanbul, at least long enough to see if she was really right about Umut.

They left the dance floor then, Umut gesturing towards a young man with a camera who seemed to be trying to get his attention, and Eve heading in search of somewhere to come back down to earth. She spotted an empty seat next to Grandma Lila, but she smiled at the older woman and kept moving, not quite prepared for the grilling that might await her there.

She spotted Meredith, sitting alone at an empty table, finding her feet carrying her over to her. "Do you mind if I join you?" she asked, nodding towards the empty seat to her right, as the one on her other side had a man's suit jacket draped over it.

"Not at all!" Meredith had a broad smile and a vaguely familiar air that made Eve feel like she was an old friend, not someone she had just met that morning. "It's Eve, right? Celia's friend?"

Eve nodded. "And you're Meredith, Poppy's mom?"

Meredith's smile grew impossibly wider as she threw back her head with laughter. "I guess you could call me that, though really I'm more of her step-mom." She leaned forward conspiratorially. "She came as a package deal with my boyfriend, who was a single cat dad when we reconnected last year. But you're right, even as I said 'step-mom,' it didn't feel quite right. I'll be Poppy's mom, at least in your mind."

"How did you end up here?" Eve blurted the question before she could consider if it was an appropriate one to ask a stranger. "I mean," she hurried to explain, "just that clearly you aren't from around here, and yet you live in Celia's building. You have a Turkish partner, a Turkish cat. Forgive my curiosity, I just can't really fathom how it all happens for all of you. I mean, you...Celia...Jasmine..."

"Well, luckily for you, it's one of my favorite things to talk about." There was that wide smile again, slipping away only when Meredith took a sip of her water. "I'm a travel writer, so I was always on the go. Istanbul was just supposed to be one stop of many, but you can see how that worked out. Adnan and I reconnected, I fell in love with

Poppy, and Celia offered me the opportunity to sublease her apartment." She shrugged. "It all fell into place, once I made up my mind to stay. Once I even let myself consider it a possibility." She gave Eve a sideways glance. "Why? Are you currently wondering if it's a possibility for you?"

"Oh, no." Eve shook her head on impulse, before considering that being honest with a near-stranger might be a good way to test the waters towards being honest with herself or her old friend. "I mean...maybe. It's crossed my mind. This is the first I'm saying it out loud. But it's too much to figure out. What are the odds an apartment just falls into your lap? And what about my job?"

Meredith shrugged. "I don't know anything about your job, so I certainly don't have any opportunities to share with you in that department." She leaned forward then. "But I do have it on good authority that the apartment across from Celia and Enes is about to be available."

Eve frowned. "Isn't that where you live? What do you mean?"

"It is." Meredith nodded. "I was downstairs in Celia's old apartment until her lease ran out and Adnan and I decided it was time to move in together in his apartment across the hall from them." Her eyes flashed with excitement. "But we—all three of us, I mean—are about to pack ourselves up into a caravan and travel around the country for a while. It seems I've written just about everything I can write about Istanbul for the moment, at least, and Poppy is just itching to go on a road trip, so..." Her voice trailed off as she shrugged. "Adventure awaits."

"Wow." Eve swallowed, her mouth feeling dry all of a sudden. "I mean, that's amazing. Congrats!"

"Thanks," said Meredith. "And don't forget about the apartment. If, I don't know...the stars suddenly align and you need a place to stay, you've got one."

Twenty

I t had been ages since Eve and Celia had been together in the apartment, getting ready for the day. Or at
least it seemed that way, in the aftermath of the ceremony, the food, and the dancing that never seemed to end.
Finally, after the desserts Jasmine had prepared had been
served—and devoured, a sure indicator that she was, in
fact, a wizard in the kitchen—the evening began to feel like
its end was nearing.

Eve slipped away to the bathroom, surprised to feel
something like sadness at the fact that the event she had
been anticipating for so long was about to be over. "This
is ridiculous," she muttered to herself. "It's not like it's
my wedding. And, let's be real, it's not like I even like
weddings!"

"Oh, you hid it well this time, but I've always known
that to be true," a familiar voice called from the last stall of
the restroom.

Eve sighed. "Celia? You heard my mumblings?"

There was the sound of a toilet flushing, followed by what sounded like layers upon layers of tulle being re-arranged.

"Uh, do you need some help in there?" Eve asked.

"Nope! All good. This is nothing compared to the hoop skirt the bride wore at the first wedding I went to in Turkey. At least I can take myself to the bathroom." The door opened then, and Celia emerged with a smile on her face. She was beautiful in her gown, a floor-length silk number that had a boat neckline and nothing like the radius of the dress she was describing.

"I did hear what you said," she said, her eyes locked on Eve's in the mirror as she washed her hands. "And I'm pretty surprised by the impression you can do of someone who's excited about a wedding. But...and you can't tell anyone this...I'm glad it's all about to be over. I'm ready for that quiet newlywed life I've been so excited about."

"I bet." It seemed as good a time as any to bring up something that had been weighing on her for days now, so Eve plowed forward. "About that, though...are you going to, I don't know...take a bit of a break from work? I don't mean just for your honeymoon, either. It just...well, it seems like you've been working yourself to the bone."

Celia nodded. "An astute observation. Enes and I were talking about that last night..." She looked down, then glanced quickly up at Eve's reflection through her lashes. "As you know, Grandma Lila didn't stay at my place last night."

Eve crossed her arms over her chest, trying to look mad, but knowing the smile on her face betrayed her. "She and I had a very illuminating conversation about that. Seems she was never even asked, because you knew full well she would have said no."

"That's true. But you don't seem to be regretting your sleepover with Umut, and you might be interested to hear what Enes and I were talking about."

Eve shook her head and made as if to cover her ears with her hands. "I'm not looking for any pointers in the dirty talk department, if that's what you're about to say."

Celia swatted her on the arm. "You know it isn't. It's about my work...my business, really. We talked about me bringing someone on, someone to help me manage it all. Maybe even come up with some new systems...an app that could solve efficiency problems for the clients that don't need the full hand-holding package. I need someone to help me do that, not someone to be overworked so I can put my feet up and eat boxes of assorted chocolates—"

"Or Turkish Delight," Eve cut in.

"Or that," continued Celia, without dropping a beat. "But a partner, really. So I can have a life outside work and so that person can, too." She closed her mouth, giving one expectant nod to Eve. "So? What do you think?"

"I think it's a great idea," said Eve. "Of course I do. I'm a huge fan of work-life balance, especially where my best friend is concerned. Any idea when you'll start looking for someone?"

Celia chuckled softly as she shook her head. "I wasn't planning on looking for anyone at all. I *thought* I was asking my best friend if she wanted to be my business partner."

"Me?" Eve had to pick her jaw up from the floor. "Really?"

"Of course." Celia nodded like she had all the confidence in the world that her friend was the right woman for the job. "So what do you say?"

Without thinking twice, the words tumbled out. "Absolutely. I'd be honored."

Twenty-One

Eve had let her feet carry her out of the bathroom and back into the ballroom, her eyes seeking Umut the entire time. Celia had given her a knowing—and dismissive—look after the decision was made, and there was only one person she wanted to talk to now.

Oh, she would talk to her brother, too. The rest of her family back home, to be sure. Just because she had spent one night in a man's apartment didn't mean he was suddenly the only person she wanted to make her decisions with.

Still, though, there was something so compelling about sharing this with him. About reading the reactions on his face as she shared her new plan with him. About confirming that, as she strongly suspected, he would want to be part of those new plans.

And if he didn't? If the news that she was going to be sticking around longer made him get cold feet and run away? Well, that didn't really matter to her either, at least not in that moment. She was that sure that this decision was the right one.

As she was craning her neck across the dance floor to where she had last seen Umut assisting one of his photographers, she failed to watch where she was going and—

"Oof! Sorry!" She stepped back from the person she had collided with, a feat that proved impossible when that same person captured her in his strong arms, pulling her against him to steady them both. "Umut!" she cried as she looked up to meet his gaze.

"We can't keep meeting like this, Eve. One of these times, someone is liable to break something." He smiled down at her, but he hadn't released her from his grip.

"Hi," was all she could say as she blinked up at him.

"Hi," he replied. "Everything okay?"

She nodded. "I'm going to come back," she blurted.

"I know." His smile seemed forced now. "It's a great city. How could you stay away?"

"No." She shook her head. "I mean, I'm going to leave on my original flight, but then I'm going to come back. Soon. On a one-way flight this time." At the confusion written on his features, she continued. "Celia asked me to work with her, and her neighbor Meredith offered me her apartment. Even *I* couldn't find an excuse to go back to Missouri after both of those offers came in within the space of half an hour."

"But...really? What about your job? Your family?"

"I'd rather work with Celia than for anyone else. And my family will understand. Especially since they'll get some quality time with me and a face-to-face explanation."

"I see." He took one long blink and then locked his gaze on hers. "Where do I figure into all of this? Am I one of the things you'll tell your family about?"

"Of course." She beamed at him. "You and Orca. And Celia and Enes and Jasmine and even Meredith, who's about to be gone. And Istanbul. My God, does this city have a lot to offer. I think when they hear about it all from me—and especially when they see the way I light up talking about it—they'll prefer to have an Eve who's living a life that lights her up and is around a little less frequently than one who's always around but bordering on sinking into a deep depression."

"That's good." There was nothing forced about his smile now, no hesitation in his features. "I'm glad it isn't just me that you're staying for, even if that sounds like the stuff out of a movie. It would be too much pressure."

She nodded. "Absolutely. And I want to give this thing between us the space to grow into something wonderful. I don't want to squeeze the life out of it before it even has a chance to become that."

He pulled her closer then. "That's good," he said again. "I didn't want to scare you away by saying that I think we have the potential to be something great, but you took the words right out of my mouth."

She stood on her toes to press one soft kiss on his lips. "I'm so glad I get to keep knowing you. This is going to be a great adventure."

"That it is, Eve." He dropped a kiss of his own on her forehead. "That it is."

Author's Note

Thank you so much for sticking with me through the Cats of Istanbul series. This has been one of my favorite series to write, both because it has let me bring my own cats' antics to the pages and because seeing this fictional community take shape has been nothing but a delight.

To stay updated on other works in progress or purchase books and bundles directly from me, please visit my website at kcmccormickciftci.com.

If you loved this book, please consider leaving a review, as that is one of the best ways to support indie authors like me. Reviews left on major retail sites (wherever you bought this book is a great start!), Goodreads, and Book-Bub will help other readers discover this book, too.

About the Author

KC McCormick Çiftçi is an English teacher turned romance writer. She spent the majority of her twenties living and working abroad, collecting the experiences that inform the stories she tells. She enjoys telling multicultural and international love stories through romantic comedy and women's fiction. She lives in Turkey with her husband and a herd of cats.

Prior to diving into the world of romance, KC published two self-help books for intercultural couples, *Loving Across Borders* and *The K-1 Visa Wedding Plan*. Both are available wherever books are sold.

For updates on upcoming releases, behind the scenes news, and all my favorite book recommendations, visit kcmccormickciftci.com (or just point your phone camera at the QR code below).

Books by KC McCormick Çiftçi

Austen in Turkey
Pride, Prejudice, & Turkish Delight
Sense, Sensibility, & the Mediterranean Sea

Home (Abroad) for the Holidays
Christmas on Inishmore
Christmas at Terminal One
Christmas by the Sea

Intoxicated by You
Intoxicated by You

Cats of Istanbul
The Vet Upstairs
From Strays to Soulmates
Whiskers and Wanderlust

Choose Your Own Adventure
We Were Inevitable

Intercultural Relationship Self Help

Loving Across Borders
The K-1 Visa Wedding Plan